an unholy triquetra

celtic fairy tales

jason parent, william meikle, and curtis m. lawson

Book 9 in Crystal Lake's Dark Tide series

Let the world know:
#IGotMyCLPBook!

Crystal Lake Publishing
www.CrystalLakePub.com

WELCOME
TO ANOTHER

CRYSTAL LAKE PUBLISHING
CREATION

Subscribe to Crystal Lake Publishing's Dark Tide series for updates, specials, behind-the-scenes content, and a special selection of bonus stories - http://eepurl.com/hKVGkr

a knot within a knot

jason parent

part 1

my nails crack against the armrest as what the pilot called *normal* turbulence spirals well beyond normal. And to think that only five minutes earlier, I wasn't afraid of flying. So much can change from just a few simple choices: deciding at the eleventh hour to attend a technology conference in Italy without my family; electing to leave that convention prematurely to catch an earlier Air France flight home in advance of oncoming weather, only for an unexpected delay on the runway and for the storm to freakishly change course into the airplane's path mid-flight; and in my haste to make my ill-fated trip, choosing not to call my wife and daughter to tell them I'm coming home and that I love them.

A *crack* as loud as an eighteen-wheeler ramming into a boulder rattles my seat. The din is coming from somewhere outside or against the plane. The lights flicker, and someone nearby squeals. Others gasp. Up ahead, a child wails. In the pause between lightning and thunder, a steady string of prayers converses with the pitter-patter of the rain.

I release a breath and look past the elderly woman to my right in the hope of catching another glimpse of the wing and its two beautifully functioning engines keeping us aloft and alive. But the shutter is now closed, blocking my view of the raging storm and the pitch-black that has swallowed the sky. An unnatural darkness blots out starlight and cabin light. Flashes of lightning are the only means to see anything out there, were there anything else to see. The woman must have closed the shutter. Maybe she saw something after all, something I don't want to see.

So I look at her instead, seeking comfort in the presence of a stranger. She is as frail as a wraith, a stick with a kindly smile. Her eyes are closed as she rests her head against her seat. Despite the lurching and jostling that sends both my mind and my stomach into an uproar, she seems to have found peace, a lonely island in the eye of the storm while the rest of us swirl in the tempest. And with each flicker of the cabin lights, her sallow skin and pronounced cheekbones illuminate. Her skeletal face permeates my thoughts like a bad omen.

The woman greeted me warmly when I took my seat beside her—I understood enough French to pick up on that—but gone now is her charity and fellowship, and my heart seizes and lungs refuse to operate as I face this storm alone. Yet her deep breaths, forcing the steady rise and fall of her bosom, emit a pulse that is soothing in its cadence, if only I can convince my body to emulate it.

And I try. Like counting off a beat, I mimic her breathing and sit back. As if aping her crests and valleys or mocking my attempts to match them, the plane also rises and falls but in much faster intervals, tickling my stomach in that nauseating way of cars on hilly roads. With each dip, the plane creaks like a rusty hinge. A strobe light bursts behind the shutters, the roar of thunder chasing at its heels. I imagine the lightning, with its dots and dashes, is speaking in Morse code. The message is clear: *You are fucked.*

A *ding* sounds, and the captain's voice comes over the intercom. Crackles and dead air break apart his words, so much so that I doubt even those fluent in his language could have found any meaning in them—or any hope.

Furrowed brows and frowning mouths confirm my suspicions as I glance across the aisle. The captain doesn't bother repeating his message in English, though the sentiment seems universal: we are all going to die.

More thunder follows more lightning, and heavy raindrops pelt our carapace like automatic gunfire. The plane gives a long groan akin to a whale song, and for a second, both metal and the meat within go silent. Even the hysterical child has lost his voice. Thinking of my daughter, thankful she is safe at home, I hope the kid has fallen blissfully unconscious. I hope the same happens to me.

The lights flicker one last time before going out, and the plane pitches downward. I curse our hubris for thinking something that weighs more than twenty elephants should ever transport people through the sky. As oxygen bags drop from the ceiling, a flight attendant bravely rises to remind us how to put them on. His tears, like crystal prisms, refract colored light, brightening his skin even as his expression darkens. A jolt knocks him to the ground, and he doesn't rise, nor does anyone move to help him.

The child's wailing returns in earnest, countless banshee souls joining in the chorus. I clench my teeth to bite back my screams. The force of our descent and my locked-up muscles pin me to the seat, my fingers clutching the armrests in a death grip.

A hand covers my mouth, and I instinctively shake it away. The elderly woman leans forward and meets my gaze, offering me that same kindly smile she wore when I took my seat beside her. Her steady hands work with a quiet strength as she pulls the straps of the oxygen mask over my head and sets the mouthpiece in place, even before putting on hers. A smile twitches my mouth. The gentleness of her act mixes with the absurdity of the orange duckbill mask to serve as a fleeting balm to a body prickling with panic.

I nod, a short bob to show my thanks. She smiles with her eyes, which gleam with the wisdom of one who has learned to accept what is beyond one's control, and rests a hand on mine. Tears warm my cheeks as I think of the wife and child I will never see again. I'm grateful, though, that I do not have to face my final moments alone after all. With an effort of sheer will, I unclench my fingers and take the woman's hand.

A blast immerses the cabin in blinding light. A *clang, clang, clang* follows, as if rocks are pelting an aluminum trash can in which I've made the unfortunate mistake of hiding. The plane dips sideways as an endless torrent of wind whooshes through the cabin, forcing my useless eyes shut. Water and what I presume to be napkins and peanut wrappers whip into my face. With them comes a moment of clarity: *this is it.*

And I laugh. The notion that sticking my head between my legs could somehow save me pushes my mind toward hysteria. I grit my teeth, determined to face my end with dignity, as if doing so would earn me the respect of a child who would never know one way or the other. I wonder if I have time to text her to say I love her, like I should have done before. But I have never squandered my affections. Both she and my wife, *they know.*

Still, I don't want to die, and I rage against the unfairness of it all. I summon more anger to displace some of my fear, slamming my head repeatedly against the headrest like a temperamental child. The howl of the wind tunnel drowns out all other sounds. My ears pop as I swallow. I squeeze the woman's hand harder and harder as we plummet to earth, ashamed I haven't had the decency to learn her name or repay her kindness.

a knot within a knot

I wake to a vacuous, white oblivion. The blurry world does not rush into focus. Light stings my eyes. As I lift my arm to shield them, a jolt of pain shoots through my elbow, following nervous passageways upward to stab my already-throbbing brain. A dull hum is the only sound that reaches my ears.

A gelatinous gunk sits over my lip. I raise my arm again—this time, it hurts a little less—and touch the warm, syrupy substance. I know it is congealed blood even before my eyes register it on my fingertips. *A nosebleed?* It can't be a good sign to wake up to blood.

I reach for my wife, comforted to find her beside me as I try to piece together the crazy night we must have had. The hangover afflicting me is worse than any I recall from my wilder twenties, and I have never been blackout drunk before. *Where did I go, and what did I do to make me so . . . uncharacteristic?* It hurts too much to think . . . or maybe to think too much. I groan and press my palms into my temples, trying to squeeze out the jackhammers in my skull and their high-pitched machinery whine. My thoughts flutter and buzz like mosquito wings. I reach for my wife again, seeking her familiar comfort, but she feels brittle and bony. Unless my full-bodied beauty has been stricken with fast-acting pestilence, she isn't lying beside me.

So who is? Could I have possibly gotten so drunk that I would betray the sanctity of my marriage? That would be beyond uncharacteristic, not me at all. I want to retch, but more importantly, I want to understand. I can't clear my head, and I can't figure out where I am or what has happened, only that this is not my bed, and my wife is not beside me. At least I sense that much—that and danger. Vomit tastes bitter in my mouth, having risen in my throat before I can choke it back down.

The sour taste helps me remember terror swirling through my thoughts and a plane falling from the sky in the dead of night. But judging by the light above, sunlight, I know the storm is over. The night is over. And I am . . . *alive?*

A fearful logic reins in the excitement blossoming with that revelation, like the threat of an accident within the thrill of a rickety rollercoaster ride. I dropped from the sky, yet here I sit, grounded, intact, I think, and somehow breathing. *When everything becomes clear, will I like what I see?*

I take a deep breath and, with it, fresh, clean air—mostly, anyway. An underscore of loosened bowels and a coppery dissidence dilutes the revitalizing aroma of earth, pine, and grass on a dew-wet morning—nature unadulterated. A draft tickles my skin, which is covered with moisture, I assume sweat. I reach up again, pain centralizing on a tender spot over my left eye. A shallow gash travels from my eyebrow to my temple, and it oozes as if already infected. A substance like raw egg makes phlegm-like strings between my middle finger and forefinger. Nausea rises within me, and I wipe the wound with my sleeve then prod it with my fingers. Though the flesh is tender, the gash does not seem to be leaking fluids.

A tug at my ear, and I claw away the oppressor with that instinctive panic that inflicts even the most macho of men when eight-legged things tiptoe over their skin. But it is only my oxygen mask dangling from my ear as if hanging from a cliff's edge. Calming, my sight clearing, I check my body for further injury. My headache relents enough to allow me to think in more than fragments. Legs, hips, torso—my elbow protests every move, but I am whole, bruised but unbroken. I'm seated in a plane that crashed during a storm, and I'm alive. *Praise God, I'm alive!*

The ringing in my head dulls to the drone of a far-off church bell. Other sounds replace it. I can hear no screams, and for that, I am thankful, but the low moans and racking sobs are not much better. The child who was wailing is now silent.

A smile shakes on my lips. A laugh escapes them, a tittering unlike anything that has passed through them before, anxious, exhilarated, and admittedly, somewhat maniacal. I turn to the woman beside me to share our mutual good fortune and gasp. She sits at peace, much as she'd been during the worst of it, but her eyes stare forward blankly. The slow rise and fall of her chest is no more. With quivering breaths, I examine her for injuries but see none, except for two clearly bent fingers, those I'd held as our heap of metal plummeted toward Earth.

Did I somehow kill . . . The thought is too terrible to entertain. My breaths come shorter, each an effort. I try to stand but whiplash back into my seat. With trembling fingers, I fumble for the belt clasp, find the button, and toss the strap from my lap, smacking the woman in her leg. Heat rises in my cheeks, even though I know she couldn't have felt it. Mystified by my own stupidity, I explode out of my seat and collide with the ceiling. The knock to my cranium is more disorienting than painful. A sudden need to escape my confines consumes me, my claustrophobia so intense that my chest cramps, and my skin seems to shrink. My fingers curl into claws under my chin as I hug myself closely and shuffle into the aisle, noticing the state of the plane and its remaining passengers despite my efforts. Both are whole at first but become less so as I shamble toward the front of the plane—or where the front of the plane once was.

I kick something that spirals a few feet in front of me: a toddler's sneaker. Turning away from the white walls, which are marred more and more by dark splatters the farther I go, I focus instead on that sneaker. Part of me knows I should stop and help those who may be injured, but my feet betray my humanity. The insectile, baser portion of my brain still choosing *flight* despite the irony isn't lost on me. I'm a good man. I want to help them. My body simply will not obey what my mind thinks is right. At least, I tell myself that. But the way the dead lie mangled, gouged, and broken, as if they ran with bulls and lost, makes me shudder at the thought of passing them, never mind providing them aid. Whatever the reason, every part of me needs to be out of that plane.

So that's where I head, gazing down at the floor. Some fatherly instinct stops me only long enough to pick up the sneaker. Fortunately, I do not have far to walk, as the carpeted aisle gives way to twisted metal then to scarred earth. I recall being jealous of those in first class, where even a man in handcuffs—likely some criminal being extradited—had been lucky enough to sit, while I was crammed into a bucket seat, but had I been in front, I can't imagine I'd have fared better. Though I suspect the worst, I pray for the other passengers. I pray more for myself.

Soil, turned as if plowed, precedes wet, shin-high grass spotted with rocky outcroppings. Lichens and stunning star-shaped blue flowers cover the mounds. A red-orange early-morning sun shines as if through a haze despite the cloudless cornflower-blue sky.

To my left, right, and everywhere else but behind me, where I am not yet willing to look, more of the same spreads out for many acres before kissing spruces and pines, the beginnings of what appears to be a massive forest. Beyond the trees, where the ground continues to elevate, snowcapped mountains stand sentinel over the horizon. I try to recall the flight trajectory from the screen in front of my seat before it flickered out. *We were heading over the French Alps when . . .*

Think. I shake my head and try to concentrate on what is important. I've survived a plane crash, so the worst has to be over, but I'm only God knows where, certainly not yet out of the proverbial woods. As if by their own design, my feet continue plodding forward, heading straight for the literal one.

Evergreens as tall as skyscrapers form a dense canopy over the entrance to a dark and foreboding place. Yet light, flickering like fireflies, subsists intermittently within that forest, dazzling and wonderful. It and the sounds coming from the same direction beckon me forward—*human* sounds of mirth and jubilee, as if a carnival is hidden within the bark.

For the first time, I notice I'm not wandering alone. Shambling and dumbstruck, much like me, a few other survivors walk with blank faces alongside me, like a small herd of zombies searching for their lost souls. A large man in a leather jacket, which is open to reveal a bloodied sweater, limps through the grass to my left. To my right, a young woman with a ponytail tucked through a ball cap takes each step as if she is on a frozen pond, and the ice is cracking. I hear the efforts of others, footfalls on rock, grunts, and grass swishing against fabric, but call to none, and none call to me. The sounds of the forest embody answers to the only question that matters: How do we continue to survive? The Pied Piper song drawing me onward fills me with wonder and warmth despite the chill and, perhaps most dubious of all, with a sense of hope.

I don't see the little girl in pigtails, who is barely more than a toddler, until she trips several yards ahead of me. Her unhappy accident snaps me out of my trance, and I run to her. Although her chin quivers, she does not cry or make any other sound as she pulls a scraped knee in to her body and pouts up at me with big, shimmering eyes. Sticking out her lower lip, she reaches up with both arms, and I wordlessly scoop her up and plant her on her feet, one of which is missing a sneaker. The other foot wears one that is a perfect match for the shoe I'm holding. Marveling at the luck, I help her step into it and Velcro it tightly.

Back on her feet, the girl bends to pick up a knit dolly with button eyes that give it a voodoo-doll look more than that of a child's toy, but the kiss she plants on its forehead suggests it is more than just a toy to her. I wonder how a creature so small and precious could find herself alone in that clearing, but we do not talk of her parents and do not search for them. Exchanging barely more than glances, nods, and uncertain smiles, we take each other's hands and continue our walk, our touch solidifying that, for the foreseeable future, I am her guardian and protector, her savior from further knee scrapes, bruises, and other injuries perhaps not yet experienced or merely not yet felt.

I'd be lying if I said her touch doesn't implant a similar sense of security in me as we step into the darkness. With my free hand in front of me, I slink forward, wary of low branches and stinging needles. I feel my grip tightening around the little girl's hand and, remembering the broken, brittle fingers of my former traveling companion, force it to slacken through cleansing breaths. My heartbeat nevertheless quickens as we trek farther into the unknown, sweet, melodious tunes promising an end to the horrors of night and nightmare: salvation.

Scents, too, carry on the breeze, the strongest being the mouthwatering aroma of meat sizzling on a spit. The warmth of its fire cuts through air now so cold that I can see my breath. And again, an underscore of rot, the stench of decomposition, of a season dying— late fall in a temperate mountain valley under a tree umbrella.

So when the warmth comes, it ironically triggers the shivering in me. My fingernails are purplish-blue, my free hand white and bloodless. I blow on it in a feeble attempt to warm it. With the fading of the shock, trance, or whatever it was that got me out of my seat and wandering into the woods, I begin to take stock of my surroundings as more than just a place but a harsh wilderness that can harm me if I don't keep my head on straight. Though we seem to be many miles away from civilization, I know that assessment to be false, unless animals have found a way to control fire and play instruments, all of which had before seemed dreamlike but now root me in reality and caution.

And the others . . .

I hasten my pace, wondering how I could have been so indifferent to those who may need my help. I'd been so self-centric, so self-absorbed that my own peril was all that mattered, even with potential salvation for all within earshot. Fear, I suppose, has dampened my reason. Even if that makes me human, it doesn't stop me from wishing I could be better. I resolve to help the others, starting with this little girl.

"Cover your eyes," I whisper as I sweep her into my arms without objection. My elbow cracks and burns as I lift her, but the pain is temporary and easily ignorable in the face of greater concerns. She buries her face in my shoulder, her dolly clutched in the crook of her arm. Whether or not she understands what has happened to her, she is managing the foreignness of me and her environment, braver than perhaps even I am, and I find strength in her strength. Again, I try not to think about how she ended up wandering the wild alone for fear my heart will break. And again, I dare not ask and extinguish her calm. Safety first, questions later.

A glance over my shoulder, and neither the plane nor the clearing is visible. The other survivors have vanished, or else I've simply lost track of them in the gloom. Something about their absence fills my very being with dread. We are deep in the forest now, the aloneness so complete and the darkness so encroaching despite the growing sounds and signs of civilization ahead and the little bundle of life in my arms, whom I squeeze tighter.

The wind tickles the back of my neck, causing the hair to stand on end. I don't belong here.

Although I can see the trees thinning ahead, I slow my pace. The girl's body trembles, either from cold or from sobbing. I draw circles on her back, trying to soothe her. Only now do I ask her name, but she doesn't answer. I spin around but see only trees looming over me every which way I turn, their branches like bony arms with long, narrow fingers reaching for me. I lose sense of direction. My palms begin to sweat. I cannot turn back now, no longer sure which way is back. My only option is to continue toward the sounds.

After only a few more steps, my breath catches in my chest. A silent cry passes my lips. A shadow stands tall before us, man shaped but not a man, gray from head to toe, with huge elk-like antlers emerging from a faceless head. Two oblong limbs, thickest where hands should be, extend from its sides. Massive and ominous, it rears up, reaching out with those unnatural appendages. I step back as it steps toward us.

I blink, trying to clear my eyes, as I know they must be deceiving me. A stag or some similar creature: that's all it can be. Dangerous, sure, and nothing a city dweller like me is equipped to handle but certainly not anything . . . unnatural. I scramble through the recesses of my mind for some nature-show tidbit that may save our lives should this animal charge. *Do I play dead? Run in zigzags?* Moving with infuriating slowness when all I want to do is turn tail and run, I put the girl down and usher her behind me. "Stay there, and don't move."

"*Bonjour!*" the beast says.

I examine it closer, confusion displacing my fear, uncertain whether the creature spoke or sneezed. "Bless you?"

"Ah, English then." The creature ambles closer.

I nudge the girl backward, keeping my body between her and this talking monster.

"Oh!" The beast raises its arms. "What a sight we must seem to outsiders." Hands emerge from the elliptical openings at the end of its limbs. They remove a cowl from its head, revealing the smiling face of a man entering his twilight years, graying hair, and crow's-feet at the corners of his eyes, which still sparkle with the zeal of the young. I see no hint of malice behind them.

I straighten. The tension in my shoulders begins to break.

"Forgive me. I sometimes forget what it was like for me when I first arrived here. The antlers are meant to honor Ankou, our Lord's great were-stag and noble servant, as we all strive to be." The man comes closer still, his arms outstretched. "Welcome and well met! Belisama has bathed you in her light, surely, for she has guided you here, out of the storm." He laughs. "And out of the sky, it would seem!"

He approaches within arm's length. I reach behind me to ensure the girl is still there without taking my eyes off the oddly dressed stranger. He wears a grayish robe akin to something a Franciscan monk might wear that's tied at the waist with a leather cord. His garb lacks any ornamentation except for the massive antlers now hanging from his back like an angel's wings. They're affixed to his hood by a hinged apparatus around his neck that resembles the visor on a knight's helmet. Old-fashioned but certainly twentieth century loafers adorn his feet.

"I have never seen a plane that large. Marvelous! You must tell me all about it."

"Please, sir. We need help. Our plane crashed—"

"Yes, I heard! Gave us all quite a fright, I assure you. Some of the young ones thought Great Balor had arisen from the sea to gobble them up, most having little notion of Balor or of the sea, as it were. They were terrified, and if I am being honest, so was I." He clasps my arms before I can flinch away. "Surely, Belisama's light shines upon you. And on the morning of Samhain! Cernunnos be praised. Truly blessed, we all must be."

I don't understand much of what the man is blabbering about, and I don't care. The little girl's parents and the others back at the plane who may still be alive are counting on someone to save them. These simple folk may be all the hope they have. "We need to help the—"

"Ah, and who is this little one?" The man crouches and reaches out toward the girl, who ducks back behind my thigh. "Hello, little sky child, daughter of the air. My name is Rainier. And who might you be?"

Receiving no response, Rainier stands. "Adorable, your daughter. A beauty to rival the summer and winter queens themselves."

"She's not my daughter. She's . . . " I lower my voice. "Her parents may still be alive . . . still in the plane." I suck in a breath and reach for his hand. "Please, sir. We need to help them."

Rainier tugs away from my grip on his sleeve, a frown dancing across his lips before departing. "Yes, yes. But first, we must help you and this beautiful child, no?" Without waiting for a response, he turns and waggles a finger over his shoulder.

After stuttering out a protest that falls on deaf ears, I pick up the girl and hurry to follow. The air grows smokier, but the light is brighter with every step. It dances like fire here and there at eye-level, as if tiki torches stand in the open spaces between trees. From them or elsewhere nearby comes an aroma like that of pork in a smoker.

"The gods surely show you fortune, leading you here on our third and final day of celebration, for the changing of the seasons is nigh upon us. Cernunnos offers you a share in our blessings. Belisama, her light. Their will be done through you and with you, so many offerings. There is much to celebrate, my new brother. The gods have called you home."

"Offerings? Home? I just fell out of the fu—" I growl but snort out my frustration. If the antlers aren't enough to give me pause, Rainier's strange ramblings are. He may be some kind of fanatic. He may be dangerous. I am not in Kansas anymore.

"Sir . . . Rainier, please. I mean no disrespect to your religion, but speaking as one human to another, there are people back there on that plane. People who need our hel—"

a knot within a knot

I stumble over a tree root but manage to regain my footing. Rainier continues on as if he hasn't heard a word I've said, and I see no other choice but to follow. The idea that I might have survived a plane crash only to be captured by some deranged cult presses on my mind like stones over a witch.

We pass the first light, and I see that my tiki-torch comparison is fairly dead-on. Except atop a long wooden shaft, two large bones cross over each other pirate-style to create a platform for a wicker cylinder that stinks of a mixture of kerosene and bacon fat. The bones look like femurs, but I am a techie by trade and have little knowledge of anatomy, so I plead with myself not to jump to conclusions. At the very least, the wicker basket's precarious perch atop the bones looks like a fire hazard.

Rainier is oblivious to my concerns and doesn't even turn to check on us as we follow him into a world lit by fire and the few trickling rays of sun that manage to breach the forest canopy. Dust motes swirl in the thin shafts of yellow light that shoot diagonally into a green-and-brown world, dying where they touch down. Lines of torches arch away at my sides, appearing to circle a small village built over rock and root. Thatched-roof cabins sit in groups around the biggest tree trunks, circles within a bigger circle, like eyes growing out of potatoes. Low branches weave in and out of the homes, the cabins either built around them or the trees permitted to grow through them. In spite of my circumstances, I must stifle a chuckle as I take in the community, for although the forest is somewhat thinner here, it remains a forest, and I cannot shake the sensation that I've discovered an elvish town straight out of *The Lord of the Rings*.

Stranger still are its people. Several men are dressed like Rainier, their cowls up and horned but no longer, in themselves, frightening. The prongs of some of the antlers appear to have been dipped in blackberry jam. At least a dozen or so women wear plain ankle-length dresses and wreaths of blue and yellow flowers resembling those I saw in the clearing. Many, both men and women, wear nothing on their feet, yet they show no sign of discomfort. The rest of the adult villagers wear an eclectic range of clothing—mostly woven sweaters and trousers—styles that seem to have outlasted time itself, never mind the age in which they might once have been fashionable. Wearing everything from flapper bonnets and top hats to bell-bottoms and capris, the villagers are certainly a long way from their Parisian counterparts in fashion and all other things.

Or perhaps they are ahead of the curve. *They say everything once in style comes back in style.* The strangeness of the era-mixing clothing, the sort of mixed Christian-pagan religious beliefs, and the unconventional habitat instill an awe within me that holds fear at bay.

The indigenous children are the most peculiar yet. Each wears what resembles a chasuble, all black with orange trim, with a pointed witch's hat on his or her head. Their faces are conversely orange with black trim, scowling eyes, and crooked mouths full of jagged teeth painted over true jovial ones, designed to match the carved turnips and pumpkins they carry. Ghastly but holiday-appropriate, I assume, having never spent time in France at all, never mind its more isolated communities.

A cheerful and friendly sort, both children and adults offer us smiles, waves, and greetings as we pass. Conversations in a hodgepodge of Western European languages ensue, my prior exposure to which having been enough to allow me to identify French, German, and Italian being spoken but not the words being said. The Scottish lilt is also prevalent, though I find those using it equally impossible to understand. I don't have to—the pointing fingers and broad smiles directed our way are evidence enough. That and the fact that several of them are speaking the Queen's English. Not surprisingly, no one sounds American.

Outside each home, fires burn in controlled pits constructed within stone circles. Up ahead another hundred feet or so, where the lines of torches enclosing the village end their outward arch and begin curving back in, a massive fire burns. A large wheel of woven twigs and dead grass, like something from a Burning Man festival, swirls at its center, a pinwheel of fire spewing heat. The head of what must have been a Guinness-world-record-setting-sized goat stares coldly from the pinwheel's center, the fire's reflection dancing across its dead black eyes. Sparks alight on the clothes of the revelers circling it, who seem unfazed and unharmed as they dance with linked arms around the conflagration. Two fiddlers, an accordionist, a few lyrists, several pipers and flutists, percussionists, and even a horn blower conjoin to play a dance tune that, with the odd ensemble of instruments, should be cacophonous but is nevertheless upbeat and melodious in the manner of an Irish jig but somehow closer to something a traveling minstrel might play in a medieval period piece, updated slightly for modern times. It's something I might hear on PBS.

"Celtic?" I ask without forethought.

Rainier stops and faces me. "This word you say . . . Other travelers have used it to describe us. I suppose it is a name outsiders have given us or perhaps to people like us. But it is not a name we have adopted or accepted. We are nameless—Gaule, if you must, though that is not a true answer. We think of ourselves only as the children of Cernunnos and Belisama. A few here were always such, exiles from northern lands, across rivers and seas, who taught the rest of us, lost souls like you, the way. My family hailed from Germany, my father a soldier who defected, escaping to these mountains during the Second Great War with the French prisoners in his care. Together, they found a new way of life here, a peaceful one. It's the only way of life I have ever known or ever wish to know, but my father has taught me of the outside world and of how ugly a place it can be." He *tsks*. "But there will be much time for stories once the wheel has turned."

He sticks out his tongue as if to taste the air then bows his head. "We give thanks to our Father, Lord Cernunnos, and his great stag, guardians of the forest, and to the Holy Mother for nurturing us, their children." Looking up, he says, "Soon, you will understand all, and you *too* will give thanks and be nurtured in return."

I am not sure if he means *also* or if he is referring to me and the little girl when he says *two*, and I do not care enough to ask. The antler-wearing apostle of God-knows-what is clearly a few cards short of a full deck. I vaguely recall a saying—something about a fool and those who follow him—and decide that I have wasted too much time prancing around the woods.

My regrets multiply when I see a naked teenager shackled to a giant boulder. My eyes were drawn to the bonfire and the celebration encircling it. I failed to notice the horrific site just beyond the fire's light. But I see it now, and I think to run, but my feet are frozen to the ground. All I can do is stare as my heart pumps faster. This place, these people—everything is all wrong. I long to return to the madness of the broken plane.

Yet my feet remain firmly rooted. Not only do I lack the courage to run, but worse still, I am powerless to help the chained boy. Blood trickles from unfamiliar symbols scratched into his chest and limbs. They remind me of hieroglyphics or another ancient alphabet I learned about in school but thought I'd forgotten. One marking looks sort of like a *C*, another like the Roman numeral for ten or perhaps an hourglass turned on its side, and still another looks like a chicken's footprint. The word *runes* comes to mind, but I am not sure I really know what that word even means other than what I may have gleaned from playing video games. I do know that the rock he is bound to reminds me of Stonehenge, especially with others like it spreading out in yet another circle, the same strange characters marking each but fortunately lacking a shackled human.

The teenager's gaze meets mine. A black smear mars his forehead as if he were a Catholic on Ash Wednesday. Sweat runs in rivulets through other black spots on his temples and cheeks. His skin is borderline red, as though he has experienced sun to a degree impossible under that greenery ceiling. His eyes shimmer with terror, yet they are not bereft of hope, as if he sees a potential savior in me. But I cannot even save myself, motionless and stupefied like the coward I am.

A crooked smile forms on the boy's mouth. He holds his head high. To my shame, I look away.

"Sh-Shackled h-human," I blubber as the wonder leaves me and sanity—if my frantic thought pattern can be called that— returns. Yet my first coherent action is to shield the little girl's eyes from the display of public indecency. I hold her close and shrink away from Rainier, casting suspicious glances at anyone and everyone beside me. Raising a shaking finger, I point at the wicked man who would harm me and this innocent child, the man who would bind naked boys to rocks and worship gods with antler helmets and fire. "Why—"

"What is the meaning of this?" His face a deep purple and his double chin wagging, the large man in the leather jacket and bloodied sweater I spotted in the clearing lunges out of the crowd, jabbing a finger at each villager he passes as he approaches the shackled boy. A wreathed woman attempts to pacify him but is dragged along by his arm. With attention diverted from me and my pathetic attempt at a protest, I feel yet another pang of cowardice as I allow him to take up the sword.

The wind changes, hitting me square in the face, and I inhale the noxious and nauseating odors of burnt hair, charred fat, and rot, this time much stronger than it was earlier and not that of decomposing plants: somewhat like burnt bacon if mixed with roadkill on hot tar. The large man, clearly British from his accent, continues to rave, but any comfort given me by the presence of another crash survivor is stifled by the smells. Another firepit at the center of the Stonehenge-like circle draws my focus. Trickles of smoke rise from dying embers. The witch children have converged around it. With stained but evidently sharp butcher knives, hatchets, and other instruments, they hack away at what appears to be a pair of adjacent goats or boars or one really long . . . *pig?* I cannot see the animal clearly. The child forms move quickly and expertly as they cleave through meat and bone then deposit carved chunks into their jack-o'-lantern containers.

My often-irrational fatherly concern for the safety of children momentarily trumps all others, and I forget about the bound teenager and the ranting Brit. "T-T-They can't eat that! Even burnt like that, it's . . . it's rotten."

Rainier chuckles. "*They* love the taste of ash. Even in death, all life must serve Cernunnos." He shakes his head and claps me on the shoulder, his belly jiggling. "I once saw them eat through an entire . . . Well, stories are best saved for a long winter. The season is at its end. Come. We must make our final preparations."

"You!" the Brit shouts, but I hardly notice.

"Who loves the taste of ash? The children? I'm telling you they can't eat—umph!"

The raving man grabs my arm and spins me around to face him. "We need to get back to the plane," he says, his breath hot against my nose as he draws within inches of it. "There are folks in need of our help. The stag . . . and these people"—he waves an arm—"they're all insane. Every last one of them."

The little girl curls into my shoulder.

"Sir, you're scaring her."

"Are you mad? Sh-She *should* be scared. They've got a lad chained to a rock like he . . . he . . . he's some kind of sacrificial lamb. And—" The Brit struggles to speak between harried breaths. "A-And they won't do anything to hel—" He steps back, his eyes wide and his teeth clenched, his chins wagging as if I had slapped him. His shoulders drop, and he seems to deflate. One hand paws at my sleeve as the other attempts to hide his tears. "It's my wife, sir. She's hurt."

When he again meets my gaze, he sees something in my eyes that ignites the flames behind his. He pushes me. "Ah, to hell with you." He reaches into his jacket pocket and withdraws a cell phone. He holds it up, apparently searching the sky for a signal.

Cell phone? I can't believe I didn't think of it before now. I check my pockets for mine, trying to recall where I last saw it, as a procession of witch children approaches. Each face remains perfectly painted to match the vegetables they carry despite their recent labors over a hot grill. They march directly between me and the distraught Brit, who is circling and cursing as he fiddles with his phone. A picture emerges in my head of the seat-back pocket and of my phone resting inside it. *Maybe he'll let me use his.*

The little girl giggles, pointing and making faces at the other children as they pass. One crosses his eyes and sticks his tongue out at her, at which she laughs so hard that she farts. I laugh, too, high and wild, in spite of it all or because of it. But I cannot shake my fear, even though no one has attempted to harm me. A naked boy being shackled to a rock will do that, I suppose.

As I try to imagine a logical reason for that outdated form of punishment—perhaps it's what passes for justice in this tiny hamlet—the large man slings his phone against the ground. "These people . . . these fucking twats. They won't help. They won't step foot in that clearing." He claws at his hair and spins, glowering at everyone he sees as spittle flies with curses from his mouth. I cover the little girl's ears.

"Why won't any of you help me?" His arms flail, smacking one of the witch children in the nose. The jack-o'-lantern in her arms teeters, and for a tenuous second, the girl manages to rebalance it. The Brit looks down at his unintended victim and shrieks, his face turning a ghastly shade of white as he swats the pumpkin from her hands before falling onto his buttocks. A collective gasp escapes the crowd as the gourd shatters on the ground, a derelict shell. The witch girl drops to her knees beside it, her mouth hanging open.

A wreathed woman cries out, rushes to the girl, and enfolds her in her arms. "Oh no, Ailsa. Your offering . . . Oh, Ailsa!" she manages between sobs.

The little girl fidgets in my embrace, her tiny arms outstretched as she reaches for the crying mother. Her efforts remind me of my own little girl, who is more than just an ocean away. Perhaps it's the universal gesture for *Let me down* that my daughter has also used a hundred times before. I get the feeling I have let my daughter down for the last time.

I gently lower the little girl to the pine-needle floor. She takes off running in that stilted, comical way only toddlers and penguins affect. After hugging the woman and the child, neither of whom seem to notice her presence, the little girl attempts to pick up the broken pumpkin pieces, but they keep slipping from her arm basket as she tries to clutch them against her chest. After a moment, she tries to assemble the pumpkin fragments on the ground, as if they are pieces of a three-dimensional jigsaw puzzle, her lips pressed together tightly with determination.

The villagers form a circle around us. Some are frowning, others scowling, while yet others are unable to look at us at all. All notions of glee and friendliness are gone. The circle closes. A hand clenches my shoulder, striking fresh fear into my heart. The woods are quiet, save for the crackles and snaps of fire and the mumblings of the Brit, whose ass is still firmly planted on the ground. His words are gibberish, for the most part, though I think he says something about fingers.

"It's okay," the girl who dropped her pumpkin says. She rises and pulls away from her teary-eyed mother.

"B-But, Ailsa . . . " She lashes a finger out at the Brit. "*He* broke it."

"And he shall fix it." Shirking from her mother's clawing grip, Ailsa approaches the large man and offers him a hand up. "Come. Let us go see if we can help your wife."

It takes a moment, but Ailsa's words seem to register. The man slowly rises. "Really? You . . . you want to help me?"

Ailsa nods and smiles.

"But won't it be—"

Ailsa shakes her head.

The Brit, now standing, takes her hand, and she leads him to the back of the witch parade. The man is clearly not in a stable state of mind. His eyes shake and shimmer in their sockets, and his chin is covered in drool. I fear for the girl, Ailsa, but catch a glance between her and her mother, who has calmed considerably. They exchange slow, almost imperceptible nods.

The circle disperses. The grip on my shoulder lessens, the change in tension reminding me that it was ever there in the first place. "Cernunnos helps those who help themselves," Rainier says, a warm smile on his face as he withdraws his hand.

"Don't you mean God? God helps those who help themselves?"

"The one and the many."

His religion and its apparent ties to Christianity confound me, and I think to explore it more with him—and particularly how it justifies chaining someone to a rock—when a boy rushes toward me—a young, bloodied, naked teenager.

I throw my arms up in defense, and he jumps into them, bear-hugging me before clapping me on the back and letting me go. "Today, Belisama's light shines on me, brother. May her light always shine upon you."

"And also with you," I mutter reflexively, not really sure why. Some remnant of a Catholic upbringing long since cast aside, I suppose. I believe in God and maybe Lucifer, but Belisama or Cummerbund or whatever these villagers worship seems crazy to me. But I'm not about to tell any of them that, imagining the pearl of wisdom I'd receive in return. *It doesn't matter if you believe in Cummerbund. Cummerbund believes in you.* Or worse, they might chain me to a boulder and carve funky symbols into my skin. A tingling in the back of my brain warns me that what is lost must be replaced.

Yet I opt for reason and sanity in a place where there may be none, acknowledging how crazy the many books of the Bible would sound to those newly introduced to it. No one has made any sort of move against me. The formerly harnessed teenager seems to bear no ill will toward me or his former captors. In fact, he is so deliriously happy that it has apparently made him impervious to the cold biting at his exposed nether regions. His life, his body sans clothing, his community . . . He seems to have all he will ever need.

I sigh. *The Great Cummerbund provides.*

I am spared from offering the naked teenager my coat by a villager who drapes a woolen blanket over his shoulders.

Wool, sheep, livestock—I don't see any animals, not so much as a bird or even a bug. "How do they live up here?" I give the young boy a once-over as I recall the odd, elongated animal the children chopped and placed into the pumpkins. My voice comes out an octave higher than normal as I ask, "What do you eat?"

The teenager and Rainier exchange glances before breaking into laughter, sharing an inside joke at my expense, no doubt. Shaking his head as his chuckling tapers out, the young man is escorted toward a well by his blanket-bearing kin. By the well, two villagers await with buckets and rags.

"Relax, my brother." Rainier's own mirth slowly dies. "You are safe now and amongst family. All will be explained to you as we winter." His eyes gleam, and he coughs as he stifles another outburst of laughter. "And you can rest assured: we do not eat people, though I hear eyeballs can be mighty tasty." His grin widens. "I jest!"

I force a smile to match his but feel no conviction behind it. "So you're not going to chain me to that rock and sacrifice me to, uh, this . . . this Cummer—"

"Cernunnos. No, brother. Our cup is brimming. So, too, is the cup we offer Cernunnos. The circle turns, light and dark, life and death. It is as it was and as it always shall be. At Imbolc, Belisama nurtures us, and so at Samhain, we give back to her paramour, who extinguishes the light so that it may burn fresh in time, blessed with new life." Rainier looks me over as if estimating my worth. "You are our guest, and you will be treated as such through the long winter. No one will harm you. Come Imbolc, should you choose to leave after learning our ways and reaping the blessings of Belisama, we will show you the way. By then, I do not believe you will wish to leave."

"Imbolc? Is that like spring?"

"Yes, your word, I believe. Our neighbors down the mountain celebrate it by eating crêpes." He shakes his head. "Very strange."

"I was thinking more like leaving today or tomorrow. Don't get me wrong. I . . . I appreciate your hospitality and mean no offense, but I've got family to get back to, and so do those people back there." I throw a thumb over my shoulder. "They need our help. Don't you have phones or computers or a fax machine . . . " I again take in the small village. The absence of wires, windmills, solar panels, running water, or any other potential power source is painfully evident. "Hell, I'd settle for carrier pigeons right about now. You must have some way of communicating with the more . . . technologically advanced world."

Rainier frowns and shakes his head. "I am sorry. All that we need is here."

"But the passengers . . . some of them may be badly hurt, but they're still alive. They're still people who need our—"

A scream splits the air, sending the hair on my neck upright.

Rainier fixes me with a solemn gaze. "It is too late for your fellow travelers. They are your gift to Cernunnos."

"My gift? I don't . . . Rainier, someone's hurt. Surely you understand that."

More cries and panicked shouts for help follow. They're not the wails of the injured but the terrified cries of swimmers circled by sharks. In the otherwise-silent air, they are as loud as owl screeches and air horns.

I grab Rainier by the front of his robe and tap my fist into his chest. "What are you doing to them?"

He slaps my hand away. "I have done nothing. The snow must be falling. The time for celebration is over. We must head inside."

"I'm not going anywhere with you!" I look around for the little girl, ready to march her straight out of the mountains if I have to. After all, *God* helps those who help themselves. But she is no longer by the remains of the pumpkin.

"Little girl? Where are you?" I search the village but see only nervous faces standing by doorways. The witch children are returning, each empty-handed. They head into cabins, ushered in by mothers and fathers standing in candlelight by open doors. Ailsa, too, returns, a skip in her step, the Brit no longer with her. Her mother hugs her before both disappear into a nearby cabin.

The musicians and dancers are gone. The screams from the clearing stop. A final door closes.

And I feel alone.

"Come," Rainier says softly, his words no doubt intended to be soothing, but I can sense the urgency behind his tone. He places a hand on my arm. "We must get inside. *They* are coming."

"They?" I shrug away from his touch. "Who"—*What?*—"are *they*?"

"Come. Please. I'll explain inside. It is not safe out here. We will be mistaken for offerings. We have already given them plenty to ensure a bountiful rebirth. There is no need to offer more."

I search his eyes for answers, for truth and fallacies, order and chaos, and the wisdom to know the difference. All I see in them is a haunting sincerity—and fear, enough to quicken mine.

Following behind him to his open door, I feel the warmth of a hearth burning inside. But I freeze at the threshold, aghast at my own neglect. "The child! Where is the child?"

I step away from the door as darkness, thick and sentient, creeps toward us from the direction of the clearing, obfuscating everything like some gelatinous, ever-expanding blob. A rank odor precedes it, like muck at low tide but cloying and choking, almost unbreathable.

"I am sorry, brother," Rainier says, his words imbued with what I believe to be genuine dismay. "Perhaps someone else has taken her in. We must hope so, for if you do not come inside now, it will be too late for you as well."

A threat or a plea? Whichever, his urgency is now patent, and it is not lost on me. Still, I must find the girl. She was in my care. She *is* my responsibility. Through fate or bad luck, she was already abandoned by those who must have loved her. I am not willing to show her the same cruelty.

As I step farther from Rainier's door, I hear it close behind me. The darkness sweeps over me like a cat's tongue, prickling my skin and sapping my surroundings of all color and vibrancy, leaving only the grays of twilight, despite the early hour. The air is colder yet somehow humid, like that of a rainforest, its touch akin to maggots squirming over my exposed skin. It instills an immediate and overwhelming impulse to distance myself from it. I fight against the urge to run and pull my shirt over my mouth and nose, swallowing down panic and vomit before they can rise and compel me to spurn a little girl in need.

A laugh comes from my left, the unmistakable high-pitched squeal of a euphoric toddler. At that moment, it's the greatest sound on Earth. I hurry in the direction from which it came, but no one is there. It comes again from my right then everywhere, as if echoing in that abysmal darkness.

"Little girl?" I let my shirt fall back into place and cup my hands around my mouth. "Where are you?" Only my voice answers back, muffled and distorted as if underwater.

What if she isn't responding because she can't? Although I was only considering that she might be mute or slow to speech, my mind quickly ventures into darker territory and other, more troubling reasons why she might not be able to speak. *Like whatever stopped the screams coming from the plane.*

Rainier's words run through my head. *We will be mistaken for offerings.*

I scoff at my fear, embarrassed for having allowed the superstitious ranting of an obviously loony zealot get to me. But I cannot rationalize away the sensation of imminent danger or the unnaturalness of the gloom.

The girl laughs again. She emerges from behind a tree not more than twenty yards away, pointing at me and giggling as if her hiding was all a game. Her other hand clutches the life out of her dolly, its dress dark and grimy. She looks up and begins to twirl under the empty dark.

No, not empty. Black speckles, like ash after a forest fire, glide down to the earth. The little girl sticks out her tongue to catch one.

They love the taste of ash.

"N-No," I mutter, the word blubbering from quivering lips. I race toward her, my arms outstretched, but trip over an outcropping of rock and smack down hard. I can taste blood in my mouth as I hastily rise. My eyes are blurry as I try to refocus on the girl.

She scrunches her nose. "Bleh!"

"Here!" a man yells from behind me. I turn to see Rainier a few steps away from his door, his arm arching upward as he throws a long, narrow object at me. An umbrella lands at my side.

Any initial puzzlement dissolves quickly, and I snap it up and fumble to open it, my gut telling me that I have to move quickly. A gust of wind swooshes past me, tickling the hairs in my nose. My gaze follows it, toward where the girl was standing, but she is gone. Her dolly sits folded over on the ground.

With another whoosh of air, it vanishes before my eyes. I sit up and sling the umbrella over my head. A black smudge stains the tip of my sneaker. As I stare at it, hoping it is only dirt, it disappears along with the sneaker tip itself and much of my toes. I suck in a breath, steeling myself a moment before the agony hits, and I scream. But pain and fear surge me to what's left of my feet. Half hopping, half heel-stepping, I hobble toward Rainier and his sanctuary, thoughts for the little girl all but forgotten.

His face ashen and wide-eyed, Rainier seems to float like an apparition, his robe blending with the darkness to make him seem almost formless. He stares at a shaking hand, still out in front of him after having thrown me the umbrella. I cannot see what captures his attention, but I can guess.

"Get inside!" I shout, but he doesn't move.

At last, as if breaking from a trance, he smiles, a sickly thing that worms over his lips. "Cernunnos has chosen me. I must answer his call." He stumbles forward on wobbly legs, away from his open door. "Oh, Great Cernunnos! I offer all that I am to the sidhs. May my sacrifice bring—"

a knot within a knot

His words meld into screams as winged creatures as large as vampire bats move with dizzying speed. They jettison Rainier into the air and out of sight with an uncanny efficiency, a swarm of piranha in a bloodlust, with only a long, decrescendoing cry to mark the distance.

I did not see what took Rainier, not truly, or my mind fights against processing it. They had thin-membraned wings and long black cords for tails with pleated ends. But one turned toward me, if only for a split second, revealing an almost-human face but with too much mouth and way too many teeth.

I hobble faster, gritting against what threatens to be debilitating agony, narrowing the distance between myself and the door. *Just a few more yards. Almost there.*

A gale rushes through the forest, and the black snow comes at me sideways.

BOUND IN THE VALLEY OF BALOR

CURTIS M. LAWSON

rent stared at his text messages, waiting for a response. His eyes darted to the corner of his cell phone screen to double-check that he had service. It showed full bars. He grunted and typed another message.

Kelly? Why the fuck aren't you answering me?

"Maybe she's asleep," Jay said.

"What?" Trent said, glaring at his prisoner.

"You're texting your girl, right? It's late. Maybe she's asleep."

"Don't you look at my phone, scumbag. Keep your eyes on the floor."

"I guess there is a six-hour time difference from here to New York, though. That would put her at four in the afternoon or so, right?"

"I said, shut your mouth."

Jay snickered and shifted in the plastic chair at Terminal Five. His handcuffs rattled the armrest and the overweight businessman sitting across from him cast a nervous glance up. Jay winked at the man, causing him to turn his eyes back to his book.

"I wasn't looking at your texts. You're mean-mugging your phone and you're typing so hard you might just crack the screen. I figure it has to be a girl on the other end." Jay paused and raised his eyebrows, looking at the Federal Agent. "Unless you're into guys. No judgment. It's the 21st century, right?"

"That's a healthy attitude to have where you're going." Trent's fingers were busy typing another angry text message as he spoke. "You got that pretty red hair. I'm sure you'll have plenty of boyfriends at Rikers."

"Nah. I'm not gonna make it to Rikers. Old Man Murphy ain't gonna let me make it into a courtroom."

Jay was right about that. As soon as Ken Murphy had gotten wind of Jay's extradition to the US, he'd pulled strings to make sure it was Trent who brought him in. Trent owed Murphy a favor or ten, and he'd agreed to wipe the slate clean if he delivered Jay to his men, rather than the feds. He didn't know for sure that Murphy was going to kill Jay, but the smart money was on that outcome.

"You could uncuff me and turn a blind eye. Say I overpowered you on a piss break. There's gotta be some karmic reward for saving a life."

Trent ignored the request and stood up to stretch his legs. It was almost time to board the plane back to the US and he was already feeling stiff. He'd spent too much time in these hard chairs, and he couldn't get up and wander around with a handcuffed prisoner in tow. That was all right. He'd get home to Queens and stretch out in his own bed. He'd be too sore to fuck, but Kelly would know he'd be expecting a blowjob, same as anytime he got home from work.

But where the hell was she? Fridays were her short at work. Maybe she was up too late and decided to take a nap. She was a night owl, after all. She claimed it came about from waiting up and worrying about him back when he worked Vice for the NYPD. Now it was a habit.

Trent hated her late nights and her daytime naps. It seemed so ass backward to him. He insisted that she come to bed at the same time as him, but she'd stay awake, playing on her phone until two or three in the morning. He'd always check her phone when he woke up to make sure she wasn't texting with another guy. If she was, she covered her tracks well. All he ever found open was the Kindle app and Candy Crush.

A voice called out over the PA system. Trent couldn't make out any of what was being said, aside from the words *Air France*, but he flew enough to know that they were boarding the first passengers, and that included law enforcement with extradited criminals. One of the few perks of escorting crooks and thugs to face good, old American justice.

I know you're awake. Do you have someone there with you? Is there another guy in my fucking house?

"I think that's us, boss," Jay said, offering his cuffed wrists to Trent.

Trent grunted and put his phone in his pocket. He unholstered his gun and handed Jay the key to uncuff himself from the chair. Nearby passengers muttered and shifted nervously at the sight of the pistol. Trent hated how sensitive Europeans were about guns.

"Uncuff one wrist, then turn around slowly, hands behind your back."

"I know the drill, boss."

Jay did as he was told, and Trent handcuffed him again, this time from behind. He holstered his gun and led Jay toward the boarding gate. The girl at the gate spoke English, and he was able to show her all the necessary paperwork without much of a hassle. A flight attendant showed them to their seats. They had lucked out. The only empty spots on the flight were at the front of the plane.

"First class, huh?" Jay asked, nodding his head in approval. "At least you know how to show a guy a good time."

"Enjoy it, prick. This is the most luxury you're gonna see for a long, long time. "

"Told you, boss. I ain't making it to prison."

"Then I guess you really had better take it all in."

Trent grunted and nudged Jay toward the window seat. Jay stretched his arms back and jiggled his handcuffs. Trent poked him in the back, urging him forward.

"Come on, man. Don't make me sit on my hands. What am I gonna do? Highjack the plane? Pull some D. B. Cooper escape? Do you think I have a parachute up my ass?

Trent took a deep breath, considering how much of an asshole he felt like being. He didn't have much sympathy for mobsters and lowlifes, or anyone really, but it was a long flight. Also, the prick had plenty of discomfort coming his way.

"You're lucky I'm a nice guy," Trent said, uncuffing Jay and letting him stretch his arms for a moment. "You make me regret it, and I'll put a bullet in you in front of this whole cabin. I don't give two shits about giving these rich fucks nightmares for a month."

"Your kindness is appreciated," Jay said, presenting his wrists to Trent so that he could be re-cuffed from the front.

Jay scooted over to the window seat. Trent pulled an old paperback out of his gym bag, then stowed the bag in the overhead luggage compartment. He tapped the book, a history of law enforcement in America, against his thigh as he checked his phone again. Kelly still hadn't responded, and he could feel his cheeks getting red. If he didn't hear from her before the plane took off he'd be out of his mind the whole flight. He hadn't wanted to call her in front of his prisoner. You never want criminals to know about your personal life, but what choice did he have?

He tapped her name in his phone book and hit call. The phone didn't even ring. Her voice chimed in almost immediately—a short greeting followed by a joke about never checking her messages before a beep. Trent hated that message. They were adults. Adults checked their voicemails and left serious greetings.

"Kelly, I'm getting on the plane back to New York. Call me back. I don't want to spend this whole flight wondering what the hell you're up to." His voice was a whispering growl. "You don't want me to spend this whole flight wondering what you're up to."

The rest of the first-class passengers started filing in. Trent got into his seat, but never took his eyes off his phone. His anger was on the rise and he found himself regretting not making his prisoner sit with his hands behind his back for the whole flight. He glanced over at Jay, hoping to find him peaking at his phone or doing something else disrespectful. Kelly wasn't there to take the brunt of his anger, and he yearned for a reason to take it out on someone else.

Jay wasn't giving him anything at the moment. The mobster was simply staring out the window. He sat in silence, with his hands on his lap and in clear view. Trent grunted at the good behavior and turned back to his phone.

He tried Kelly's cell phone again. It went straight to voicemail, and he punched the seat in front of him. A bald man in the seat in front of him looked back, casting a confused glance at Trent. Trent gave him the meanest cop-glare he could muster, and the man turned around without a word.

More passengers filed into the plane. After first class was fully boarded, Trent could hear folks at the back of the plane bustling into their seats and wrestling with their carry-on luggage. He was thankful that he wasn't stuck back in one of those cramped seats for the long flight. His anger at Kelly still grated on his nerves, but at least he had some legroom.

Trent lost track of how many more times he called Kelly while waiting for the plane to take off. The phone never rang. She never answered. Each time he was met with that stupid, childish message of hers. He'd make her change it when he got home, he decided.

A flight attendant approached Trent and said something in French. Her voice sounded pleasant, and she was smiling, but Trent had no clue what she was saying, nor did he care. He shook his head and waved her off as he dialed his wife.

Jay looked over at the flight attendant, flashed the sort of charming smile that so many lowlifes master, and replied to her in her native tongue.

"She's asking you to turn off your phone. The plane's getting ready to take off."

"Fuck," Trent muttered, listening to the phone ring and ring. He held up his index finger and said he needed one minute.

"Sir, we must ask you to turn off your phone," she said, this time in accented English.

"*Une minute*," Jay said to the flight attendant and gave her a shrug that seemed to say *I'm sorry about this guy*.

"I'm about to hold up this entire flight if you don't call me back," Trent muttered into the phone. "All these people are gonna have their days ruined because of you. They are gonna miss connections, be late for weddings, or jobs, or whatever the hell they're flying for. Call me back."

He hung up the phone and turned to the flight attendant. He flashed his badge and asked her to tell the pilot that he needed to wait to take off because he was waiting on an important call. FBI business, he insisted. The flight attendant said that she would pass on the message.

"*C'est un connard, mais il a un badge*," Jay called out to the flight attendant as she walked toward the cockpit. She turned back and smiled at him.

"What did you just say to her?"

"Just flirting," Jay answered.

Trent inhaled deeply and tapped his foot against the floor. He watched the minutes change on his phone and sent a barrage of furious text messages to his wife.

After 20 minutes had passed, the flight attendant returned. She looked at Trent and tilted her head in an apologetic manner. He knew what she was going to say before she could get a word out.

"We have to go. I get it," Trent said with a sweeping gesture of his hand.

Trent typed out one last message, as the flight attendant waited for some kind of response.

I have to shut my phone off. Have fun with whoever you're screwing in my bed while I'm at work. I hope you're happy, bitch.

Trent shut off his phone and slid it into his pocket. The flight attendant thanked him, and Jay offered some verbal nicety to her as she walked away.

"Awfully worldly for a red-headed thug from New York. Hiding out in Italy. Speaking French to flight attendants. Real man of the world, huh?

"Everyone should speak a few languages. As for why I ran to Italy? I love the food. The wine. The women," Jay said, gazing out the window. "I also figured you geniuses in law enforcement would be too unimaginative to look for me in Florence. Figured you boys would be spilling cheap beer on your Brooks Brothers suits while scouring every pub in County Cork before hitting up the continent proper."

Jay wasn't completely wrong. The circumstances around his extradition were suspicious. Someone had dropped a dime, and Trent wondered if Murphy had double-crossed the poor bastard for some reason. Maybe Jay was running his mouth. Maybe he'd given it to one of Murphy's side pieces. It didn't matter to Trent. The details were above his pay grade.

Trent opened his book to a dog-eared page toward the middle. Jay glanced at the book and made a face at the title before turning his gaze back out the window and onto the skyline above the runway. The engine came to life, sending vibrations through each of their seats.

"Last chance to let me go, brother," Jay said, his hand pressed against the glass. "You could save a life. Big points with the man upstairs."

"You keep saying shit like that—like I've got some big moral failing I need make up for. You think you know me? You think you know what I'm about?"

"I think anyone who carries a gun to work is gonna have a hard time getting past Saint Peter. That goes for cops and crooks alike."

"I don't need to score any points with The Lord." Trent didn't raise his eyes from his book. "You might consider saying some prayers though."

A flight attendant stood at the front of the plane, demonstrating the proper method of buckling a seatbelt while pre-recorded instructions played. Trent focused on his book, paying the woman no mind. Jay, on the other hand, gave her his full attention, wondering how many more beautiful women he'd see before he got shipped off to Rikers or one of Murphy's boys ventilated his torso with 9mm holes.

Once the flight attendant was done with her demonstration, she walked up and down the aisle, checking that tray tables were up and passengers were buckled in. Jay flashed her his most charming smile as he tugged on his seatbelt for her. Trent did the same but barely acknowledged the woman.

The engines grew louder and louder and the plane began to roll down the runway. Jay thought about how he'd been a free man, just 24 hours ago. Not just a free man, but someone important—a dangerous man with money and women. Now that was all gone, and not because of anything he did or didn't do. He'd been a good soldier—loyal and obedient to the Murphy family. None of that mattered, now. He knew too much and had become a liability.

Without warning, they were off the ground. Jay watched the earth recede before him and he took a hard swallow. They'd be in New York soon enough, and he'd be dead shortly after.

The thing that had once been a man woke up beneath the black waters of a darkened grotto. It knew that it had lost everything. It was all there in the streaks of blood and bits of gray matter that floated in the water and stained the sunken earth—its dreams and secrets and sins. Even its name was lost to it—a word etched in stone, now ground into sand.

The last remnants of air drifted from its lungs, bubbling in the water and rising away, like the life that had been taken from it. Cold water filled it, in lieu of fresh air. It didn't mind. Neither the cold nor the touch of liquid in its lungs caused any discomfort.

The burning fire in its stomach was a different matter entirely. The flame was a source of suffering which had followed it into death. That pain would never cease. It knew that, and not just because the fire flared and pulsed, even in the deep, cold water. The dead man knew it as the caterpillar knows to enter chrysalis.

Standing was difficult at first. One of the creature's ankles was twisted and sat at an awkward angle. The corpse tumbled this way and that. Some mechanism that dictated balance for the living had been destroyed in it, and its body had not yet adapted to the new processes which kept it animate. It fell and thrashed about, like a baby fawn, but quickly found its footing.

Something called out to the dead man. The voice it heard was deep and terrible and it spoke in the language of earthquakes and grinding stones. *Sluagh,* it called. That's what it was now—another bit of knowledge that came to it as instinct.

Bound in the Valley of Balor

The voice implored the dead man to stay. In this place. In this world. In this life, even if life no longer graced its form. The *sluagh* could not refuse. Its free will lay somewhere in its spilled blood and the wreckage of its brain.

The *sluagh* took stock of its new reality. Pink light from the fire in its belly cut through the dark water and bathed its pale skin with a hellish cast. It reached up, touching its ruined head. The back of its skull was caved in, hunks of loose skin attached to shattered bone.

It tore away the hanging flesh and discarded the broken fragments of its skull. What was left was sharp and ridged—a jagged crown of exposed bone. This was fitting, the *sluagh* decided. In death, it had joined the ranks of the noble and ancient. Yes, it was a servant to those who came first. There was no doubt about its place. But even a slave to Balor was a king to the rest of the world.

First, there was pain. Before consciousness. Before recollection. Before fear or panic. Just agony, pulsing through the void of sleep.

Next, there was sound. Something whimpering nearby. The whistling of the wind. A slow, wet drip.

Trent opened his eyes. He was still in the plane, but the plane was not in the air. Bodies sat crumpled over in seats, unmoving. Some looked like they were unconscious. Others had expired. The drip he'd heard was coming from a young man across the aisle. The man's head leaned against the seat in front of him, and crimson droplets fell from his shattered face into a pool of blood beneath him.

Trent's memory was foggy. Glimpses of the crash played out in his mind, but they were impossible images. Lightning flashes painting the sky white and giving a sense of anthropomorphic illusion to the storm outside. Gray clouds reaching out, like the arms of giants, battering the fuselage. Deafening thunderstrikes— the roar of some hateful and destructive god.

Then there was the feeling of vertigo when the plane first lost control. He was overcome by a dizzy sense of inertia that pressed his back into the seat. His nails scraped and dug into the handrest. Somehow he could hear that sound of scratching against plastic over the cacophony of the storm, the screech of twisting metal, and the chorus of terrified screams.

He remembered seeing the flight attendant, the one that Jay had charmed with his smile, flying through the air, like a drunken superhero. She screamed, but her cry tapered off quickly, like the whine of a sports bike speeding by on the highway.

And then there had been the sensation of falling—that helpless feeling of gravity dragging you earthward as if you're caught in the invisible mechanisms of some incredible and merciless machine. Thinking of it made his stomach flip all over again, and he belched up a mouthful of bile.

He didn't remember hitting the ground. Maybe the g-force had knocked him out. Perhaps his mind had blocked out the trauma. Whatever the reason, he was grateful that he couldn't recall the impact.

Trent took stock of his pain. Each breath caused a sharp sting in his side. His head pulsed with agony. One eye was swollen shut, to the point of blindness. The tendons in his neck throbbed with inflammation.

He embraced each terrible sensation. Pain was temporary, and it meant he was alive.

Trent's hands trembled as he tried to unbuckle his seat belt. Agony pulsed through his middle finger as it pressed against the metal release. He raised his hand and tried to move the suffering digit. It was crooked and immobile. Grunting, he unbuckled himself with the opposite hand.

Pressing his feet against the floor of the plane, he tested his legs. He could put weight on them without much pain beyond what he'd normally feel after a long flight. He was still dizzy and shaky and when he tried to stand straight he fell forward against the seat in front of him. It took him a moment to realize the plane wasn't level but pitched forward.

Trent gained his balance and stepped out into the aisle, holding onto his headrest for stability. It was then he realized something was wrong, beyond the obvious. His prisoner was gone. Maybe he'd been thrown out of his seat and tossed around the cabin.

Trent looked around, scanning the dying and the dead. A few pretty young women with expensive jewelry sat broken beside each other a few seats ahead. A middle-aged man, his face a crimson mask, was trying desperately to wake his wife, despite the impossible angle of her neck. A musclebound pretty boy—some body-sculpted euro-trash type—sat weeping, his legs crushed by the seat in front of him. There was no sign of Jay.

Bound in the Valley of Balor

He checked for his gun and his keys. Both were gone. He muttered several curses and punched the baggage compartment. If Jay was alive and if he somehow got away, Old Man Murphy would have his ass. It wasn't just that he wouldn't get out from under Murphy's thumb. No, the old gangster would leave his head in Queens, dump his torso in the Hudson, and mail his dick to his mother.

He had no choice but to find Jay. How far could the prick have gotten? A mile or two? Trent's aching ribs throbbed at the thought of walking half that.

It was hard climbing out from the wreckage of the plane, the floor angled as it was. He steadied himself on headrests and the shoulders of dead passengers as he walked, the pain in his neck and ribs forcing him to pause now and again.

Ahead of him was the jagged exit wound, where the front of the plane had sheared off from the other half. The moon shone through that egress, set against the black night. Stars shined in numbers so abundant that Trent did not recognize the sky above. The few stars and constellations which shone on the clearest of New York nights were lost in the shimmering tapestry above him.

A person called out for help—a soft, gasping voice. Trent looked back and saw someone reaching out for him. They muttered something in another language, over and over, urgency in their tone. Their eyes held a plea for help which Trent could understand despite the language barrier. He turned from them and continued down the aisle.

Trent got to the edge of the wreck, where the plane had split asunder. Wires and tubes and bits he couldn't identify shown like the innards of some eviscerated animal.

Trent hopped off the edge of the plane. He landed on wet grass and soft earth. The storm-soaked mud sucked at the soles of his shoes. He grunted at the pain jumping down had caused.

It hurt to move his neck, so he walked in a slow, tight circle to survey the crash scene. A few more corpses lay strewn about the ground—folks who had paid no mind to the seatbelt light and found themselves thrown from the plane. Trent examined each corpse. Jay was not among their number.

The plane had crashed in a valley, not far from a riverbank. Craggy Mountains, silver in the starlight, rose to the heavens on all sides. The soft babbling of the water and the calm of the idyllic scenery stood in absurd contrast to the chaos of Trent's situation.

While Jay was nowhere in sight, Trent spotted footprints leading away from the plane. Trent thanked the good lord for the muddy earth.

Balor was restless after ages of slumber, and the mountain creaked as he stirred. The old king issued commands. His voice was like the crumbling of mountains, clear and audible, even below the water. The dread king called for the *Sluagh* to seek those who had fallen from the sky and bind them to this valley with the chains of death.

The *sluagh* did not question its orders. It kneeled in the center of its king's massive palm and pressed its cold lips to stony flesh—a wordless show of allegiance. Flashes of another time flickered in what was left of its mind—movie reel snippets of kissing rings and committing violence at the behest of evil, old men. It didn't recall feeling remorse then, and no sense of guilt plagued it presently for what Balor commanded.

Life beckoned the *sluagh*. It could see and hear better than it had in life, but those senses were second to its eldritch ability to feel the draw of living things, like a shark sensing prey beneath the sand.

Fish and frogs and a dozen breeds of insects filled the grotto. It was an odd panoramic sensation to feel their presence, all at once. There was something larger nearby as well—its life essence more robust than the creatures native to the cavern.

The *sluagh* looked up from the bottom of the grotto. Neither the darkness nor the water impaired its vision. A man rested in the shallows, near the cavern wall. His heartbeat, quick and strained, reverberated through the water, distinct from Balor's stirring.

There was something familiar about this man. The *sluagh* felt that it knew and hated him—that he had committed some grievous trespass against it in another life. It trod through the water, toward the human, eager to drag him beneath and watch the life escape his eyes.

No, that would be too easy. It wanted to heap suffering upon the mortal. It imagined tearing into the man's stomach and dining on his viscera as he watched. The monster wondered which would be sweeter, the taste of the mortal's blood or the sound of his screams.

The *sluagh* trudged forward across the grotto floor. Tiny fish skittered at his approach. The fire in its stomach revealed the layers of death that lay settled beneath the water. Bones and shells littered the mud. Chitinous scavengers fought over dead flesh, eager to pick the corpses clean before the patient but hungry water dissolved it all.

Ahead of him, the man crawled forward on his hands and knees. The *sluagh* watched as he vanished into a small tunnel like the vermin he was. The *sluagh* followed.

Trent had been following a series of footprints along the riverbank for miles, despite the catalog of pain that he was experiencing. The night was bright from a full moon and the sky full of stars, so he didn't need to sweep around with a flashlight to follow the tracks. Protocol and good sense dictated that he should have stayed at the crash site and waited for a rescue team. He should have helped the survivors and been a leader. He certainly shouldn't have taken off with the only flare gun and a bag full of other vital supplies. He had to do whatever it took to catch Jay, though. Otherwise, he was as good as dead.

There was also a matter of pride. No one got away from Trent. Kelly had tried to leave him a few times and it hadn't worked. Lee, that snitch who'd been squawking to internal affairs—he hadn't been able to escape Trent either. His record for bringing in the bad guys was nearly perfect.

He checked his phone for a signal for the fifth time. Still nothing. Wherever the plane had crashed, it was well beyond civilization. Where the hell in 21st-century Europe wasn't there cell service? Weren't those genius tech billionaires supposed to have the whole world connected by now?

Sure, he wanted his phone to be working so he could call for help, but that wasn't the main reason. More importantly, he needed to hear from Kelly—needed to know she wasn't getting drunk with her sister, letting the miserable bitch put ideas about leaving in her head. He needed to know she wasn't shacked up with another man in their bed. His mind went to Craig, a scrawny hipster who worked a cubicle over from her. His name came up just a little too much in their conversations and Trent was sure the prick was trying to get in his wife's pants.

He muttered a few swears under his breath and kept walking along the river. The water was rougher here than it had been at the crash site. The current broke against rocky mounds that pierced the surface, causing white foam to form atop the black water.

He wondered how far Jay had made it. How much of a head start did he have? Minutes? Hours? With any luck, he'd find the scumbag cold and stiff from blood loss or trauma. Maybe he'd find the bastard torn apart by a bear, or a wolf, or whatever wildlife lived in this valley.

There was something terrible and primal about this place, and he could picture the soil being hungry for blood—coaxing it from open wounds or urging wild beasts to spill the life of prey animals into the dirt. He looked at the lush hills, leading toward the gray mountains. Even in the moonlight, Trent could see how rich and full the grass and leaves were on those hills. He wondered how much death it took to keep them so green.

His eyes drifted to the river and the whitewater foaming against ancient rock formations, smoothed by the subtle powers of time and erosion. How many creatures had been dashed against those rocks by the callous current? How much of the riverbed was made up of bone and scale and death?

Images of the crash played through his mind again. The storm had seemed so much like a living thing—an elemental titan that might battle a handsome war god on the big screen. Everything in the valley held that sense of primal awe—enormous works of nature, in possession of a haunting sense of life. He felt it all around him, in the distant mountains, the furious river, and the ravenous soil.

Trent was a fan of mythology and battlefield literature. He was prone to wax poetic about war and bloodshed. He had a fascination with the circular, violent nature of life, but he wasn't one to give credence to superstition. The river was just water. The mountains were just rocks. The storm had been nothing more than currents and cold fronts and all the things he'd forgotten from eighth-grade science class.

He tried to block distracting thoughts of cheating wives and malevolent storm clouds so that he might focus on the tracks in the mud. The valley narrowed about two klicks northwest, and the mountains tightened up around the river. There'd be caves there, all sorts of nooks and crannies that vermin might hide. That's where he'd find his prisoner.

The *sluagh* walked from the depths of the grotto into the shallows. Water poured over the ridges of its ruined skull and from the blazing hole in its stomach. The flame burning within it flared at the kiss of oxygen in the open air.

The human was out of his sight, but the *sluagh* could sense him in the tunnel ahead. It wanted to spill the mortal's blood in tribute to Balor. It wanted to strip his warm flesh and grind his living bones between its teeth.

The *sluagh* fell to its hands and knees. It crawled into the tunnel, following the stink of the human beast. White stone shone between mud and dirt and took on the pink tone of the fire in the *sluagh*'s belly. Veins of some darker mineral spiderwebbed through the tunnel.

When the *sluagh*'s hand touched one of those veins, it recoiled in pain. Smoke rose from its fingertips and palm as dead flesh sizzled, revealing the bone beneath. It tried to push forward, despite the pain, but whatever that darker material was, it burned like acid.

Hissing and cursing in the language of its king—a language it had only known for the few minutes since it had been reborn— the *sluagh* backed out of the tunnel. It could not pursue the human through there. There were other mortals to hunt, however. It could feel them farther away, beyond the cave, and deeper into the valley. It would seek them out instead.

It turned around and walked toward the ledge that overlooked the grotto. The water rose to its waist, then to its chest, and finally, it was underwater. It strode through the water as easily as a man might walk through fog.

Upon reaching the ledge, it searched for handholds so that it might climb. It gripped the stone with little effort, finding purchase on the slightest indent or nub. Its fingertips easily held its weight, and it climbed with the quick sureness of one who needs not consider death.

Following the narrow passageway out of the cave, the *sluagh* stepped into the night. The moon bathed the valley in a cool light that made the white mountains glow like polished silver. Nightbirds cried and insects called out, but never too close to the *sluagh*. They fled at its approach, and none dared to be caught in the light of the fire that burned in its stomach.

The *sluagh* followed the draw of life across miles. The sensation was not as strong as it had been with the mortal in the cavern, but it knew the life force in the distance to be human.

Flashes of memory surfaced—the vaguest breed of déjà vu. An echo of bygone pain where the mud showed signs of someone limping through. Memories of thirst at the sight of the river. The *sluagh* paid no heed to these things. They simply didn't matter.

The *sluagh* didn't tire as it followed the scent of life through the valley. It never grew impatient or frustrated at the time it took to reach its prey. It didn't fear that which might be lurking in the night.

Orange smoke shone in the distance, painting the night in Halloween tones. The *sluagh* followed the vaporous beacon across miles, to a crater where half an airliner lay in ruins. It circled the twisted wreckage, stopping at the shattered cockpit. It sniffed at the uniformed men behind the broken glass and considered their ruined faces and contorted limbs. They were dead and had been for hours. There was life nearby, however. Weak heartbeats and labored breathing called out to it.

Sheets of metal that had broken away from the plane formed a lean-to against the fuselage. Twigs and sticks burned nearby in a firepit fashioned from debris. Two men and a woman huddled beneath the leaning metal. One of the men was young with a slight frame and big glasses that reflected the light of the fire and the moon. The other man was older with a complexion like spoiled cream. Both of them were asleep. The woman was awake and her eyes focused on the makeshift fire pit, but her mind was someplace else—lost in daydreams or memories.

The exhaustion and anxiety of the survivors was palpable. Even the two who were unconscious shifted and moaned in uneasy slumber. They shivered miserably, whether from trauma, cold, or fear, the *sluagh* didn't know, nor care. The very existence of the humans offended the monster. Their bodies radiated a warmth that it was envious of. It could feel the embers of hope smoldering in the hearts of each—a disgusting naiveté.

The woman let out a mousy squeak when the *sluagh* came into view. It skulked between the white and grey smoke of the campfire and the rising orange cloud of the nearby signal grenade. The fire in its stomach lent an outlandish glow to both.

She slapped the sleeping men on either side of her. They shot up and looked around. The man with the glasses caught sight of the silhouette shambling toward them. The older man with the sallow complexion glanced around, confused and unaware.

Fueled by hate for the living, and urged by the orders of its king, the *sluagh* broke from its clumsy shamble and rushed toward the mortals. It moved with a speed it didn't realize it possessed, gliding just above the ground. The tips of its waterlogged oxfords whipped through the tall grass. The fire within it flared hotter and brighter, blackening the earth as it passed.

The woman and the younger man scurried out through the back of the lean-to. The older man was slower, and the *sluagh* tackled him to the ground. Agonized screams reverberated off the metal wall of the makeshift shelter, as the dead thing clawed at the man's face with filthy nails and exposed bone from where its fingertips had burned away.

Fire spread, from the *sluagh*'s midsection to its victim's clothes. Within moments the man was immolated by pink flame. The smell of burning hair, melting nylon, and cooked fat filled the air. The man struggled, but Balor had granted the *sluagh* inhuman strength. Thrash and scream as he might, there was no escape. Sickened by the pathetic screams of the human, the *sluagh* pushed his chin up and punched him in the throat over and over, until his windpipe collapsed and the noise ceased.

It stood, leaving the corpse to sate the fire's hunger. The other mortals were fleeing. The *sluagh* would have laughed if it could. Where would they run? There was no escape. They were part of the valley now—nutrients to be broken down to nourish the earth and the forgotten kings below.

Gripping a sheet of aluminum from the wreckage of the plane, the *sluagh* flung it like a discus. It spun forward, forceful but unbalanced. It made a whining, wabbling sound as it sped through the air. The jagged corner stuck into the woman's back, perfectly severing her spine. She collapsed with an ugly thud that her partner hardly acknowledged before leaving her to die. Her body would have been lost in the tall grass, but the sheet of metal stood up from her corpse like a grave marker.

Life still radiated from her, though it was weaker now. The *sluagh* charged her and placed a foot on her back. It pulled the piece of wreckage from her body and brought it down where her neck met her shoulders. Her head came free of her body and a torrent of blood splattered off the airplane debris.

Only one of the trio remained—the thin man with the spectacles. He ran away, almost leaping with each stride along the river's edge. He was fast, but the *sluagh* was faster.

It took almost no time for the *sluagh* to be upon him. The two collided and tumbled into the river. They were immediately swept up in its current. The human struggled to free himself from the *sluagh*'s grip. He held back screams of agony, as the fire in the dead thing's midsection scorched him and caused his skin to blister, even in the cold water. He squirmed this way and that, throwing elbows and smashing his head into the monster, all the while trying to stay above the water. The blows did nothing to deter the *sluagh*. It held the man tight, letting its weight drag him below.

The human thrashed as they sunk to the riverbed and the current swept them forward. Their bodies smashed against submerged rocks and the human's last breath was forced from his lungs. Water filled the void in his chest, causing him to choke and convulse. All rational thought was lost to desperate instinct. The *sluagh* held him tight, against the rocks and beneath the river, until he stilled.

Leaving its victim to sate the appetites of any aquatic scavengers, the *sluagh* planted its feet against the current and lumbered toward the bank of the river. It emerged, water cascading down its grotesque body, and sizzling into steam around the flame in its belly.

The *sluagh* could still sense human life nearby . . . weak, but there. It returned to the crash site and a voice echoed from the wreckage. The intonations and the flavor of the language it spoke were familiar to the *sluagh*, but the meaning of the words was lost to it—another aspect of its old self, left in the depths of the grotto.

The ruins of the plane were angled with its nose dug into the earth. The *sluagh* climbed into the open end of the fuselage, where the front of the plane had sheered from the back. It was darker inside the plane than it was beneath the moon and stars, but the monster barely noticed.

Someone was crying out in desperation, struggling in a seat

toward the front. The *sluagh* made its way down the aisle. Corpses filled the seats on either side—skulls caved in and necks broken. No life radiated from anyone, save for the man toward the front.

As the *sluagh* came into view, illuminated by its inner flame, a more profound level of panic overtook the seated man. He screamed and pounded on the chair in front of him, tears streaming down his cheeks. When the *sluagh* came to stand beside him, it realized that the man's legs were ruined, pinned by the seat in front of him. The other mortals had tried to escape, as moot as such attempts were. This one couldn't even entertain such a notion.

The *sluagh* watched the trapped man for several moments. It wasn't sure if he was trying to bargain for his life or to make threats and challenges. It didn't matter. All were foolhardy gestures. He belonged to Balor now, just as everything in the valley did.

Heat from the *sluagh*'s burning stomach singed the man's hair. He tried to pull away from the flame, but the monster grabbed him by the head and pulled his face into its blazing stomach.

The tracks that Trent followed had gotten sloppier the farther he went upriver. The stride had shortened and the right foot had begun to drag. Jay, or whoever had left them, was hurt. This was good news. It meant he'd be too preoccupied to cover up his tracks as he moved away from the river and toward some hiding place in the mountains.

Trent was right in his assumption. As the footprints strayed away from the river and became a bit harder to make out, there were other signs of human passage. Flattened bits of tall grass where a foot had dragged. Drops of blood on broad-leafed weeds. A filthy handprint on a rock where someone had stumbled and caught themselves.

Maybe Jay had thought that no one would come looking for him. Most people would have probably left him to the mercy of the valley, given the circumstances of the crash, but Trent wasn't like most people.

He wasn't sure what he'd do when he caught up with Jay. There was the matter of the gun, which he had to take seriously. Also, he was hurt badly and in no real condition to fight, but all evidence suggested Jay was in bad shape as well. He'd figure out the details when the time came. Right now, all he had to do was find the son of a bitch.

Trent followed the trail for some time, losing it and picking it up again, until he came to the entrance of a cave. It was tall and narrow, more like a fissure than a mouth. He wondered how deep it went. Not far, he guessed. Jay was probably huddled a few yards inside, his back against the wall like a wounded animal.

Now he needed a plan. If he just stormed in Jay would shoot him dead. The guy ran around with Old Man Murphy. Presumably, he was no stranger to violence. Worse still, Jay was in survival mode. The mobster knew if Trent brought him stateside he'd be dead. What more reason could you give someone to pull the trigger?

Trent leaned against the cliff face to the left of the fissure and listened to his breath. It was loud and labored. He tried to fight back the pain that erupted with each breath, but it was no use. Some things you couldn't just will away. His breathing would be audible in the cave. It might echo and reveal him, but he had to take the chance.

Judging by the trail he'd left, Jay was in rough shape too. He was bleeding and dragging his foot. He'd be making noise for sure. Hell, by this point the Mick bastard might be passed out and snoring.

Trent poked his head into the entrance of the cave and listened for any sign of his quarry. There were noises, but none that he'd expected. At first, he thought it was a growl, maybe some sort of wild animal, but the longer he listened the more he knew that wasn't right. It was more like something grinding—stone being dragged across stone.

More subtle noises played beneath. A crunching sound, like gravel being poured. The pop and hiss of damp wood on a fire. The creaking moan of something hard and firm splitting beneath enormous pressure. Trent couldn't guess the source of such noises.

It was dark inside the cave. Trent had wanted to try and sneak up on Jay, but his labored breathing and his need to see made that impossible. He had taken two different kinds of flares from the plane. One type fit in the flare gun and was meant to be fired. The other was more like the kind of road flare you use for car accidents. He pulled one of the latter from the bag he'd taken from the plane and lit it. Setting it on the ground, he took a moment to load the flare gun as well. It wasn't a 9mm, but it would have to do.

Trent held the flare gun behind his back and the signal flare in front of him with the other hand. He entered the fissure. It was terribly narrow. He didn't suffer from claustrophobia, but the tight quarters made him uneasy. If gunfire erupted, he'd have nowhere to hide.

The cave floor was caked in mud. Tracks, just like the ones he'd been following from the crash site, led deeper in.

"Jay!" he yelled. "Don't shoot. I'm unarmed."

No one responded. The only sound was that chorus of grinding, creaking, and popping.

The grade of the cave steepened abruptly and Trent nearly lost his footing. He reached out for the earthen wall, and the flare fell from his grasp. It rolled away, farther down the cave's decline, taking its pink radiance with it.

Trent stifled a curse, then considered the advantage this might give him. He waited to see if anyone opened fire on the approaching radiance or if some savage creature waited with gnashing teeth. Neither scenario unfolded, so he followed the rolling flare, but kept a respectable distance.

The narrow cave went deeper than Trent expected. He followed the flare down the steep grade for some time, until it vanished into a chasm or off a cliff. He couldn't be sure which. Its disappearance was followed by a splash, several seconds later. There was water near, and it was a bit farther down.

Trent lit a second flare, still keeping the gun behind his back, and made his way down the path. The pale, red light tinged the walls on either side of him with a hellish tone. Insects skittered from the light, and shadows squirmed in place, like animals with their legs stuck in a snare. Even so, the flare barely cut through the darkness, but it was enough for Trent to see the ground in front of him and make sure he didn't roll his ankle on the uneven ground.

The path came to a stop, where the first flare had vanished. The cave opened up to a vast chamber. At first, all Trent could make out past that ledge was blackness, then he saw wavering reflections of the pale red light—rippling color against a body of liquid darkness. Maybe it was the hit he'd taken to the head, but it took Trent a moment to realize he was looking at water, rather than something otherworldly.

He wondered if he'd lucked out. Maybe Jay had tumbled down there and drowned. He needed to know for sure, though.

Trent held his breath and listened. The grinding and cracking noises he'd heard as he entered the cave echoed louder in the grotto. Another sound could be heard in the breaks of the cacophony. A heavy, panting breath. It was the sound of struggle and pain.

"I know you're in here, Jay!" Trent winced, trying not to let the pain show on his face. Yelling hurt his ribs more than he'd expected it to. It was even worse in his neck. He'd never thought about all the muscles that went into something as simple as raising one's voice.

"And I knew . . . " Jay's voice was soft but coarse, and it echoed through the chamber like a child's rubber ball ricocheting against the walls of a tiny bedroom. " . . . you were dirty."

"That's a serious accusation,' Trent said. He was quieter this time, hoping not to elicit the same level of pain as his last words had.

"Drop the act, Fed." Jay's voice was strained. Trent suspected he had been seriously hurt in the crash. "I don't care how crazy you are. No cop's gonna . . . "

Jay was wheezing now. Trent glanced around the cave, trying to pinpoint where in the darkness he was hiding.

"No cop's gonna climb out of from the wreckage of a plane to track down an extradited thug. You're on Murphy's payroll."

"You must have hit your head, or maybe the blood loss is getting you, Jay. I'm one of the good guys."

Trent kicked a pebble off the ledge and listened for it to hit the water. It took longer than he would have liked to hear the splash. He wondered how deep the water was and if he was going to get hurt worse by jumping down there.

"I'm your only shot at getting out of here. I'm coming down there. Let me help you."

Something exploded in the darkness. The noise was amplified to incredible levels by the dimensions of the cavern, and it drove the pain in Trent's aching head up to eleven. His legs forgot themselves and suddenly he was on his knees, leaning over the edge of the path.

"That was your only warning shot," Jay cried from the darkness. "Go back to the plane . . . go back to your girl . . . and tell Murphy I'm dead."

Oh, I'll tell him you're dead, all right, Trent thought.

It took great effort, but Trent stood up. He looked out over the field of black before him and he threw the flare as far as he could manage. He followed the flare's aura as it arced across the grotto. The water glittered beneath it, like liquid ruby. Then there were rocks, or maybe stalagmites, jagged and wicked, in a rough semicircle around a patch of dry land. It looked like the palm of a fossilized giant. There, in the middle of the rocks, Jay came into view. The flare and its light passed by him before Trent could assess the man's condition, but he knew where he was. Better still, without the flare to betray his position, Trent was now invisible.

He pressed his body low to the ground and waited, in case Jay decided to fire again. After a few moments, he was satisfied that he wouldn't be shot just yet. He rose into a crouch and tucked the flare gun under his belt. He swung himself over the cliff's edge. He'd planned on hanging, then dropping into a controlled fall to minimize any damage. His pain didn't care about his plan, however. Once his arms were extended, his breath came short and the pain in his ribs caused him to lose his grip.

Trent splashed into the water and sank below the surface. It was shockingly frigid and caused his muscles to tense. Beneath the water, the cave's ever-present grinding noise was muted, the way that all sound is when one is submerged, but he could feel its vibrations rippling through the water.

The grotto was deeper than he'd expected. His feet never hit the bottom and panic overwhelmed him as he considered how deep he'd sunk. Desperate, he struggled to swim back up. He burst forth from the water with an audible gasp.

Before he could get his bearings, Jay fired again. The shot hadn't come anywhere near Trent, but the echo of the blast overloaded his senses with a wave of pain like he'd never known before. Once the throbbing in his head had receded enough so thoughts could once more form, he dove beneath the surface and swam toward the center. He moved slowly, like the injured animal he was, but at least if there was more gunfire, his ears would be better protected.

Jay shouted something, but the words were muddled by the water and drowned out by the noises of the cave. It didn't matter what Jay was saying. The time for talking was over.

The abyss below Trent receded and he was met with a hard and slimy surface underneath. He breached the water and his fingers struggled for purchase on slick rocks. His knees pressed against the grotto floor, slipping on muck and scraping against jagged stone and the shells of dead crustaceans.

"I hear you splashing around. You could have just left me alone . . . told Murphy I got sucked out of the plane or something." Jay broke into a coughing fit and Trent tried to pinpoint the source of the sound in the dark. "Now we're both gonna die here."

You're half right, motherfucker, Trent thought to himself. He continued forward and the water receded further, giving way to mostly dry ground. He was on that island in the grotto, which meant Jay was within yards of him.

Trent retrieved the flare gun from the back of his pants. He prayed it still worked, despite having been submerged. He was pretty sure it would. The road flares had stayed lit underwater.

"At least that girl of yours makes out in all of this." Jay's voice descended into laughter. "She'll get a fat life insurance check and be free of your insecure, possessive ass. Probably won't be a week until she's taking some other asshole cop balls deep in her."

"Shut your fucking mouth!"

Trent's scream was followed by another gunshot. The pain from the sound was so intense, that he momentarily thought he'd been shot, but the slug had missed.

Stupid! He chided himself. *This prick is trying to rile you up and throw you off. Don't let him get in your head.*

"Maybe old man Murphy will take care of her for you. Stroke her cheek and tell her what a good soldier you were. Let her cry on his shoulder, while his hand drifts south."

Stay cool. Trent gritted his teeth so hard they felt like they might crack. *Let him talk. Follow his voice.*

"Those stacks of cash he keeps around are a hell of an aphrodisiac. Sure, he's old as dirt, but I hear he pops Viagra like candy. "

There he is . . .

Trent raised the flare gun and fired in the direction of Jay's voice. The flare sparked to life and rocketed forward. The fire went dark in an instant, but terrible screams, the worse Trent had ever heard, echoed throughout the grotto.

Trent stayed low following the noise, and then he could see the faintest bit of light—a floating ember, thrashing in darkness. He didn't realize what was happening at first, but then it hit him. The flare had not only found its mark, it had penetrated Jay's body and was burning inside him.

He'd thought the flare would have burned Jay and maybe knocked the wind out of him. He never expected it to pierce the flesh. It was a terrible way to go. No one deserved an ending like that.

A burning smell wafted over to Trent. It was a wretched potpourri—the chemical smell of the flare mixed with scorched hair, cooking flesh, and smoldering cotton. What made Trent cringe, however, was the layer of excrement in that juxtaposition of scents. It wasn't just the foulness of the smell, but what it insinuated. The flare must have hit Jay in the stomach and buried itself in his guts. All Trent could imagine was the boiling waste leaking into the rest of Jay's viscera.

The terrible screams went on and on. Jay suffered and suffered, but death would not come for him. No one deserved an ending like that, Trent decided. He walked toward the burning dot and felt around for Jay's squirming body. His hands sought Jay's head, and he gripped him by a shock of hair. Trent brought Jay's head to his chest and hushed him, then slammed his skull against the stony earth. It made an ugly thud the first three times Trent drove his head down. The sound was different on the fourth strike. There was a wet quality to it that sounded dreadfully final.

Trent's hands were suddenly warm and wet. He was no stranger to the feeling of blood on his hands. He'd been in plenty of fights over the years, both on and off duty. He'd put men in the hospital, ruined their smiles, and left them scarred. He'd even shot a few people over the years. This was different, though. He'd never killed someone with his bare hands, before.

He didn't feel guilty, exactly, but the surge of adrenaline and the wet touch of so much blood sickened him. His stomach flipped and he feared he might vomit. The smell of burning fat and boiling shit didn't help ease his nausea, nor did the sizzle of the flare and the pop of wet, boiling insides.

"Well that's one problem solved," Trent said.

Trent pulled his phone out of his pocket, hoping it would turn on, despite being submerged in water. Murphy would want some proof of death. A photo wasn't ideal, but it was better than nothing. His phone wouldn't turn on, however. Murphy was going to have to take him at his word unless he wanted to send one of his guys to fetch Jay's body from this cave.

Trent leaned back against one of the stalagmites and allowed himself a moment of rest. Everything hurt. His banged-up ribs. His scraped hands and legs. His throbbing head and swollen eye. He was alive though, which put him ahead of the curve for his present company.

He looked at his dead phone and his mind drifted to Kelly. He wondered if she had actually been sleeping when he'd called and texted or if she'd left him again. It didn't matter. He wouldn't have to scare or threaten her this time. She'd come to see him in the hospital when got back. Her heart would break at seeing him all battered and bruised, and he'd play on her sympathies. She was an easy mark for that sort of thing.

He put his phone away and fumbled around Jay's body for his gun. He found the barrel, still hot from being fired. He flinched and cursed, before reaching for it again. His hand darted forward and back, probing for the grip rather than the hot steel.

Trent needed to find a way out of the cave, and he knew he wasn't going to make it back up the way he came. Maybe there was a way to climb back up to the ledge over the grotto, but he was in no condition to make it up there. He'd have to find another way out. He was out of flares, so he'd have to do it blind.

He rested his back against a stalagmite to consider his options. A sudden awareness overtook him. The constant grinding was getting louder and the earth beneath him vibrated like bass through a speaker cabinet. A sense of vertigo washed over him. He attributed the dizziness to the pain in his skull and the stress of the situation until the stalagmite he leaned against began to curl around him.

He flung himself away from the gnarled tower of mineral deposits and slammed into another stalagmite that was curling inward, in the same manner as the first. They creaked and moaned as the ground wobbled like the floor of a carnival funhouse.

Trent tried to crawl away from the stalagmites, but they had all curled around him, trapping him in their grip. Suddenly, he was wet again. The ground was rapidly sinking below the water. He scrambled blindly for some opening and crawled over Jay's corpse, the torso of which still sizzled and burned within.

The water was up to Trent's mouth. He took a deep breath through his nose, afraid that it might be his last. Hands out, he followed along the stalagmites which had formed a cage around him, desperate for some gap in the bars.

Bound in the Valley of Balor

A wave of panic overtook Trent as the water rose over his head. He pressed his feet against the ground and pushed against the stalagmites. His feet slipped against the stone, denying him leverage. Giving up on breaking free with brute force, he returned to searching for some gap that he might slip out through.

The sounds of gravel and grinding stones were loud, even beneath the water. They sounded closer and more pronounced, as if he were right beside the source of the sound.

White starbursts exploded in the otherwise black space around him. His lungs yearned for air and he felt that he was being dragged deeper into the water. The disorientation brought on by pain and panic, from the inky darkness and the frigid water, and the impossibly shifting earth left him unsure which way was up or down.

Unable to hold his breath any longer, the spent air burst forth from his lungs. His breath came out in choked puffs. He would have to inhale soon, and when he did his lungs would fill with water.

Trent's body began to thrash and his arm shot out, finding a space between the stalagmites. He fought back his panic and commanded his body to do as he willed it. His fingers gripped a gnarled edge and he pulled himself through the gap. His feet kicked, first against the stone and the stalagmites, then against Jay's corpse. A moment later he was free, floating in the cold, dark water.

He kicked his legs and made wide strokes with his arms. The darkness was so complete that he couldn't see the surface and he prayed that he was swimming in the right direction. It took all his will to fight against the insistence from his lungs that he breathe.

Trent's limbs slowed. He was ready to give up and accept the inky, black death that would fill him. That's when his head breached the water. He gasped, loud and violently.

Trent paddled through the dark water, his tired, aching body barely capable of keeping him afloat. He shivered and his muscles twitched. Maybe it was from the cold. Maybe it was adrenaline. Probably both.

He didn't know which way he was swimming. Any sense of direction he'd had was now lost. He only knew that he was moving away from that sunken island that had tried to drag him beneath the water.

The sounds of grinding stone that permeated the cave, and which had seemed so much more pronounced to Trent while he was underwater, were growing in volume and intensity. The water was coming to possess a slight wake and Trent could feel the lower-end vibrations in his stomach.

The source of the noise was indefinable in the echoing space. It sounded as if the whole cavern were coming to life. Trent thought there had to be some kind of geological event underway—an earthquake or the forming of a sinkhole. That was the only explanation for the island collapsing into the grotto. The thought left him with a fear that the whole cavern might crumble atop him and that he'd die there, entombed with the scumbag mobster he'd just killed.

Anxiety pushed Trent to swim forward—to keep moving until he found an exit or hit a wall. Panic was the enemy, however. He'd seen many succumb to it. Farm-boy soldiers losing their cool in a desert firefight. Twitchy cops opening fire on unarmed citizens. Perps running into oncoming traffic to avoid arrest. Luckily, Trent knew how to combat panic. He used the same techniques he'd learned in anger management. He trod water and took several deep breaths.

Focused on remaining calm, Trent tried to take in his surroundings as best he could. It was dark—pitch black— save for the dying, pink embers where the discarded flares burned beneath the water.

A cool breeze brought a chill to his wet skin. He muttered a curse, then gasped in realization. There was air movement in the grotto, and not coming from the direction of the ledge. That meant there was another way out.

Trent embraced the cool air washing over him as he worked to pinpoint the direction it came from. Goosebumps erupted across his flesh, from the chill and the excitement of a potential egress from his nightmare situation. He swam in the direction of the breeze, hoping whatever earthen corridor carried it would be large enough to accommodate him.

He swam forward and his fingers eventually grazed the stony floor of the grotto, signaling that he'd reached some shallow part of the cavern. It was shallow enough that Trent could kneel and keep his head and shoulders above water. He slumped forward and let his shoulders sag. The ground trembled beneath him, and he feared that it might retreat deeper below the water as the island had. Regardless, he needed rest, even just for a minute.

Trent caught his breath and tried to clear his mind—tried to push back the pain in his head and his ribs. He was no stranger to suffering. His father had been a brutal disciplinarian and his military service had hardened him further. Life was hardship. You just work through it and hold on to what's yours at any cost.

A subtle noise joined the cacophony of the grotto. It was a bubbling sound, like boiling water. Trent looked behind him, *instinct being ignorant of the darkness.* One of the pink embers flared up in the depths of the grotto—a pulsing flame that burned in defiance of the water.

The flame began to move, stumbling through the deep water like a drunken lobster. Trent didn't know what was happening, and he didn't care to find out. Pushing through his pain, he stumbled through the shallows, following the kiss of the breeze. The depth of the water lessened, and Trent came to an opening. Feeling around the edges, he could tell that it was broader than the sliver of an opening that he'd entered the cavern through, but not nearly as high.

Trent crawled into the small tunnel, shuffling forward on all fours. The floor was muddy and littered with loose pebbles that dug into his palms and knees. The harsh grinding of stone that permeated the grotto was dulled in the tunnel. Still, he could feel the earth tremble and shift below him. Small stones and clumps of mud fell upon him, shaken loose by whatever phenomenon was impacting the cave system. Trent's stomach clenched as he imagined the tunnel caving in on him and crushing his body to a pulp, or worse still, leaving him trapped to die of hunger or thirst.

The grade of the tunnel was a subtle incline, and it twisted like a coiled snake. Trent crawled along a wide, sweeping curve in the tunnel. At first, he thought the dim light penetrating the darkness ahead of him was a trick of his mind. He moved forward toward it, like a thirsty man rushing at a mirage that his rational mind knew would yield no water.

He reached toward the radiance and his hand came into view, filthy and bloody. There was a way out. He was going to make it. Trent scrambled ahead, clawing and kicking at the ground to propel himself forward. The tunnel brightened more the farther he progressed until he saw an opening ahead.

The tunnel opened to an expansive cavern, several stories tall. This chamber, like the one below, was largely flooded, but the water rushed through fierce and powerful—a raging, subterranean river. A massive piece of oxidized steel stuck out from the water. At first glance, Trent mistook it for a rusted I-beam, but it was cruder than that. More so, it didn't appear to be supporting anything. Looking at it with greater attention, it reminded him more of a gargantuan railroad spike or the snapped blade of a giant's sword.

Moonlight shone through a single hole—a perfect circle, set near the top of the cave. Dust and dirt danced like fairies in the sharp lines of moonbeams. It took a moment for Trent to realize that the stone with the hole in it was not part of the cave. It was the wrong color—darker than the rust-streaked grey and white rock of the cavern walls. Adding further to the geological contrast, this portion of the cavern wall was smooth and beveled, like the cracked face of an ancient colossus whose features had been eroded by time.

That's what it was, Trent realized. A statue of some terrible cyclops whose head blocked the way out of the cavern. Its nose was sharp, with bump upon the ridge, and mineral deposits clung to its cheeks like a patchy beard. He wondered how far the colossus stretched beneath the river and deeper into the cave system. Was it just a head, or was there an enormous, sculpted body the size of Lady Liberty stretching down the deepest pits of this strange underworld?

He didn't think there were statues of that size from the days of Europe's antiquity. Its scale reminded him of ancient Egypt or a set piece from a bygone sci-fi flick, but what did he know? He was no archaeologist, and he wasn't particularly interested in the thing's history.

Trent scanned the room, looking for some other way out, aside from the hole in the statue's face. He knew he'd never be able to climb its smooth, rounded surface, even if he wasn't hurt. There had to be another option

The river came into the chamber from a tall, dark tunnel, but it flowed too powerfully for him to consider swimming upstream. The water left through a much shorter exit way. Trent didn't think there would be enough height there to even keep his nose above the water.

Bound in the Valley of Balor

He was exhausted and felt himself on the verge of resignation. He could wait here, but even if a rescue team showed up for the plane, they'd never find him in this cave. Taking his chances with the river didn't seem like a better option. Drowning on one hand, exposure and starvation on the other. And if neither of those got him, he was still concerned that the whole cave system was about to collapse on top of him.

Seeking a place to sit and think, Trent found a large, flat rock in the corner of the cave. It wasn't quite big enough to stretch out on, but he was able to curl up on it and rest while he tried to figure a way out.

His mind drifted to Kelly. He wanted to blame her for this. If she'd just picked up her phone, he wouldn't have delayed the takeoff. Maybe they would have narrowly missed whatever had caused them to crash. Butterfly effect and all that, he thought.

He wondered where she was right now and who she was with. Was she laughing and getting hammered with her sister, hatching some scheme to leave him again? Was she in mid-coital betrayal, getting railed by some other guy in their bed? Was she thinking about him at all?

"Bitch," he muttered to himself while imagining her in the arms of another man. He clenched his fists and closed his eyes. It took only seconds for his exhaustion to brush his anger away and for sleep to overtake him.

The black of the sky gave way to dark blue as morning threatened to overtake night. The *sluagh* knew that daytime was the province of the living and that the approaching sunrise would greet it harshly. It needed to retreat underground, to the pit where it had been born and where its king was bound to the earth.

There was also the matter of the final survivor—the last of those humans who had fallen from the sky. Balor had commanded the *sluagh* to end each of them—to bind them to the valley for eternity. This was the *sluagh*'s function—the reason Balor granted it life beyond life. It would not fail.

Its trek back to the caverns was much quicker than its journey to the site of the plane crash had been. It had learned things about itself in the time between. It needn't shamble on a broken ankle or clamber across hills on all fours. It could glide over the land with a smooth celerity—an uncanny gait in line with its newfound nobility.

The *sluagh* raced against the rising sun. It made its way toward the white mountains, downriver—toward the earthen sepulcher where King Balor lay restless and waiting. Vermin and rodents fled the tall grass as the *sluagh* approached. Bats and nightbirds would not fly above it. The grass turned brittle and black as it passed over. It was as if vegetation chose to die rather than suffer its presence.

When it reached a narrow break in the mountains that led to the grotto, the *sluagh* paused. Despite its newfound mastery of its body, the monster knew that it could not pass through the tunnel where its prey had fled. There was something anathema to it in the stone there—some vile mineral that burned so much worse than the terrible fire in its belly.

The ground shook and the mountains groaned. It was the voice of Balor, calling the *sluagh* home. Just as it could now glide across the earth, the *sluagh* could climb steep surfaces with ease. It clambered up the rough stone wall of the mountain, following the vibrations of its master's voice across craggy ridges and over treacherous peaks. All the while, the sky above took on lighter hues. The last blue remnants of night were barely holding out against purple and orange hues breaching the horizon.

Cresting a small peak, the *sluagh* spied the back of Balor's head, bound in place by the mountain itself. It was enormous, incredibly so, and crowned with jagged stone and lightning-scorched trees. A hole was bored through the back of the king's skull.

The *sluagh* approached the head of Balor with all the reverence that his former self might have shown to Christ arisen. It dared not lay a finger on Balor's hard, stony flesh, fearing that doing so would be an act of profanity.

The mountain rumbled—Balor giving the *sluagh* his permission to place its hands upon him—urging it to climb upon his skull and slither through the hole in his head. The dead thing did as it was bidden, gripping Balor's crown of wood and stone and crawling through the cavity bored from the base of the god's skull, through his brow.

It halted at the end of the narrow passageway. There was a cavern on the other side, formed from pale stone riddled with rust-colored veins. Resting on the other side of a river that passed through the chamber, was the mortal who had gotten away. The fire in the *sluagh*'s stomach flared as did the hate in its heart. It didn't know nor care why it hated this man so much more than the other human beings it had killed. It was simply compelled to strip the life from him.

A light flashed, waking Trent from his unintentional slumber. He'd only been vaguely aware of the pain he was in as he slept. Consciousness brought it all back with merciless intensity. He opened his eyes and popped up with a start. He was still in the cave, but it was brighter—there was a strange illumination, lending pink overtones to everything around him.

He looked up and gasped. A fire burned within the hole at the brow of the monumental statue. The flames were no natural color, but the surreal pink of a signal flare.

Trent's eyes adjusted and he realized that it was more than just a flame set in the statue's face. Some burning creature was crawling out from the hole. It looked like a man, but filthy and broken, with a fire blazing in its center. Wet, copper-colored hair hung over the creature's eyes. It wore a filthy button-up shirt that was burned away where the fire in its belly raged, leaving blackened edges of cotton around the blazing wound.

Instinct pushed Trent to retreat against the wall. He grabbed his gun and fired at the monster. A slug hit it and knocked it back into the hole, but only for a moment. Undeterred by the burning lead in its chest, the thing launched itself into the cavern, clearing the river in an impossible leap. It landed with feline grace, its palms slapping against the cave floor, followed by the balls of its feet.

Smoke wafted up from the monster's hands and feet. With a hiss, it stood tall, then hovered just over the ground. It glared at Trent from the edge of the river. This close, Trent could make out the thing's face. It was Jay. Trent had killed the man, just hours before, but here he stood, his skull open like a cracked egg and a fire burning in his viscera.

The dead thing glided toward him, malicious intent written across its face. He cursed and fired again. The slug caught the creature's shoulder, knocking its arm back but leaving it largely unbothered.

Trent tried to move further away, but his back was to the wall. He fired twice more. The shots found their mark, but the creature rushed forward, undeterred. Its speed was incredible. Trent barely rolled out of the way when it careened toward him, its hands striking out like talons. Stone chipped away from the force of the blow and sparks flashed where the exposed bone of the dead man's ruined fingertips struck the cavern wall.

Stumbling on his heels, Trent fell on his ass. Before he could raise his gun and fire again, the dead man was upon him. It tore the pistol from Trent's hand and tossed it to the far end of the cave. The clatter of its landing was lost below the roar of water and the sound of creaking stone.

The monster lunged on top of Trent, pinning him to the ground with its knees. Its touch was ice, yet the heat from its flaming stomach was terrible and intense. A sound echoed from its chest— a mockery of laughter that Trent felt more than he heard.

A bony finger pressed against Trent's cheek, then dragged down like a dull knife. His flesh opened, more torn than cut. The creature's finger kept moving down, toward his throat. Images of Kelly flashed through his mind—that incredibly beautiful face he might never see again. Those happy memories morphed into ugly imaginings with a quickness. Trent pictured her in bed with another man, doing things she had promised before church and state only to do with him.

The rising anger urged him to fight back. His hand fumbled for anything he might use as a weapon. The best he could find was a piece of loose stone, roughly the size of his fist. Trent gripped the rock and swung it up into the dead man's face.

An ugly gurgle passed between the creature's lips and water drizzled from its mouth. Its cheek was smoking and a red blemish spiderwebbed across its face. Trent swung again, catching the thing with a strike to the jaw. Its flesh sizzled and smoked, and it swayed on top of Trent. A third strike knocked the monster off him and sent it falling back.

Trent had fired his pistol into the evil thing several times, and all his shots had been moot. Yet somehow this simple piece of stone had sent the thing falling back. Trent scooted across the cave floor and away from the horrid being before him.

Sunlight was beginning to fill the chamber, bringing the current nightmare into clearer focus. Jay's broken form rose and stared at Trent with soulless eyes. Water, blood, and brain oozed from the monster's ruined skull.

Bound in the Valley of Balor

Trent glanced at the rock in his hand. Bits of flesh were burned to the stone where rusty iron deposits shone. The wounds on the creature's face, blistered and charred, were a crude approximation of the rusty lines marring the stone.

Lifting the rock high into the air, Trent went on the attack. He smashed it down into the dead man's face and atop its jagged, broken skull over and over. His broken ribs and aching neck only allowed him to hit so hard and for so long, however. His speed and stamina waned, and the monster's hand lunged up, grabbing his wrist. It squeezed and flicked its arm, breaking Trent's wrist as easily as one might snap a twig.

Trent screamed and the rock fell from his limp hand. Cold fingers clenched his throat, crushing his windpipe and summoning white starbursts in front of his eyes. Consciousness began to fade. He'd undergone too much trauma over the past hours to be able to fight back any longer.

Accepting his fate, Trent closed his eyes and imagined Kelly's face, willing it to be his final thought. That's when the ground beneath him heaved and the sound of creaking thunder filled the cavern. Trent opened his eyes and followed the monster's gaze upward.

The sun sat perfectly aligned with the hole in the statue's face, transforming it into a cyclopean nightmare with a single burning eye. The cavern shook again, and the head of the statue rose, breaking the mountain which held it on either side. Rocks cascaded down, rolling into the raging water. The river churned like a storm-tossed ocean and the iron beam that stuck out from the water trembled. A shower of rust fell from the beam and into the water below.

A single, guttural word issued out from the chest of the living corpse.

"Balor . . . "

A terrible grimace—a living, animate expression of rage—overtook the statue's face. Its chin rose above the water, then its neck and shoulders. One of the walls and the floor beneath it exploded into a hail of stone. A massive arm rose from beneath the ground. Its hand was easily large enough to crush a man between its stalagmite fingers.

The arm continued to push through the ground, cleaving the cavern. The massive hand reached for the iron beam and clenched.

A growl like exploding artillery threatened to deafen Trent. He watched in awe and the monster watched in reverence, as the titanic thing which he'd mistaken for a statue pushed against the iron rod and rose up further from the water and from below the cavern floor. He could now see that the iron beam went through its chest—a giant stake pinning it to the earth.

No matter how it moved its head, the sun stayed in the center of the statue's face, as if it had snatched the fire from the heavens and claimed it as its eye. The light that poured forth from that eye was focused and white hot, like sunshine through a magnifying glass. Its gaze left scorch marks on the cavern walls and any vermin caught beneath it were reduced to ash.

Struggle as it might, the statue, or the giant, or whatever the hell it was, could not free itself from the iron rod in its chest. It bellowed out words in a language that sounded like the grinding of tectonic plates. The dead man snapped to attention and lunged for Trent. It caught him in a bear hug and pulled him tight against the fire in its stomach.

The living monolith slowly spun its head to the side, drawing its deadly gaze toward the two of them. Trent watched the stone walls blacken beneath that focused light, even as he cried out because of the agony of the dead man's burning touch. He tried to break away and run, but either he was too weak, or it was too strong.

Trent leaned into Jay's undead embrace, willing himself to fight through the burning pain, then threw himself backward. The trick worked. The monster was thrown off balance and Trent escaped its grip. He collapsed to the floor, just before the statue's gaze was upon them. The terrible light did not immolate the living corpse but caused its skin to blacken and shrink on its bones. Its red hair sizzled away into charred fuzz. Its eyes boiled and popped, then drizzled down its cheeks.

Trent didn't waste his time watching the fate of the dead man caught in that light. Instead, he rushed toward the river, keeping as low as he could. He knew that if the statue's gaze fell upon him, that would be the end.

He made it to the river's edge and leaped in, praying to whatever god might listen that the current wouldn't smash him right into the calcified giant. The water was cold and it sucked the breath from Trent's lungs. It frothed chaotically to and from the god-thing's thrashing. The current immediately swept him away. As the edge of the cavern chamber approached, Trent dove beneath the water and held his breath, unsure if he would ever draw another.

When they found Trent, in a circle of rocks on a beach in Ireland, there was no explanation for how he had come to be there. His doomed flight had crashed over the French Alps, and the front of the plane, where Trent had been seated, had never been found.

Trent never told anyone the truth about what had happened. He skipped over the mysterious valley when giving his report to his bosses. As far as he was concerned, it was all a nightmare or a hallucination. He might have told Kelly about it if she'd been there when he'd returned home. She was gone, of course, just as he knew she'd be. She hadn't had the courtesy to so much as leave him a note. She simply packed her shit and left.

There were those who were concerned about what happened, most notably Internal affairs. It was a curious circumstance, which coincided with the disappearance of a key witness in a high-profile case against one of America's most notorious mobsters. This raised a lot of eyebrows in the bureau and caused internal affairs to uncover connections between Trent and Murphy. There was no hard evidence to prosecute him, but it was enough for Trent to be pressured into taking early retirement.

Trent had been unable to deliver Jay to Old Man Murphy, but Murphy was willing to accept that Jay died on the plane, at least until contrary evidence presented itself. Since extenuating circumstances had prevented Trent from completing the job, Murphy didn't hold him accountable for it, but he also didn't cut him loose like he'd promised to. That was just as well, Trent supposed. Working for Murphy was messy and dangerous, but it paid well, and he needed the income since he wasn't with the feds anymore.

It had been several months since he turned up on that beach. In that time, he'd used his skill as an investigator to track down Kelly. She hadn't told anyone where she was going this time. Not her mother or her sister or the friends she used to party with before they got married. She had meant to stay missing this time.

Careful as she had been, the modern age made it nearly

impossible to vanish, at least for an honest civilian. There were bank records, IP tracing, image-finding software, and a dozen other dirty tricks that could be used to track someone down.

She had done a good job this time. Trent had to admit that. Did she really think she could leave him though? She belonged to him. There was no escape.

Trent sat in his car, parked by the shore on the North Carolina coast. Kelly was waiting tables at a beachside restaurant a block away. His plan was simple. He'd wait for the joint to close, then stroll up and tell her it was time to come home. He didn't know if she'd fight him on that, but he was prepared to take her home by force if it came to that. He had a stun gun to knock her out if he needed to and a Glock for any fuck buddy she might have who wanted to play hero.

The time on the dashboard said 12:45 am. It was time to walk over. He stepped out of the car, rehearsing what he'd say to her. He'd practiced it a lot, trying to merge charm and intimidation. It was a trick he used as an agent as well. Be cool and dangerous. If someone didn't respond to one, they'd respond to the other.

He walked along the beach, his adrenaline already pumping. There weren't a lot of people out, but enough that there might be a problem if Kelly caused a scene. That was okay. He'd never minded conflict. He kind of enjoyed it, truth be told. More than that, he was excited to see the look on Kelly's face. First, there would be shock, then fear, and finally resignation. The resignation was his favorite— the way her shoulders would slump and the fire would fade from her eyes. It was like crushing her soul in the palm of his hand.

As he walked toward the restaurant, a little seafood joint called The Clam Shanty, a strange light caught the corner of his eye. Trent turned his head toward the water. The ocean was a black sheet, stretching out forever, the horizon lost between the dark water and the ebony night.

Something was alight in that black sea, spoiling the perfect darkness of the water—a spot of pink light, glowing beneath the ocean's surface. It bobbed with the tide, but moved ever forward, toward the beach.

Trent's lungs tightened and he struggled to breathe. His limbs trembled and his knees gave out. Vertigo overtook him and the world spun around him. He fumbled for his pistol and struggled to flip the safety.

There were cries of concern from other beachgoers. One teenager threw his girlfriend over his shoulder and ran for his car. An old man pulled out his phone and dialed the police. Trent didn't notice any of them. The light in the water had reduced him to a shaking madman kneeling in the sand. He pointed his gun toward the water with a shaky grip.

Everyone else had fled by the time the thing stepped out of the sea—a walking corpse with a broken skull and a pink flame burning in its center. Its charred skin was the same color as the nighttime ocean and its eye sockets possessed a shade of black even deeper within them.

Trent aimed his gun, fully aware that the bullets would have no effect. He cursed and threatened—moot gestures that were more instinct than anything else.

Trent knew that the creature meant to take him back to that nightmare valley where it had died, and he, too, should have. He knew that it would never rest until it presented him at the stony feet of that imprisoned god. He knew there was no escape.

a knot within a knot

jason parent

part II

It's my time *to die.*

Meh. I breathe easily in spite of this likelihood. Surely, I have lived. I have loved and been loved, have cherished and been cherished, and have known someone wholly who knew me fully in return. I have known the truth of another, found his center, and discovered myself there while he found himself with me.

But Marco is gone now. I am no longer whole. I am empty. So as I travel home to be with the family I left so many years ago, a home I know nothing of, I do so without joy or sorrow, excitement or bitterness. No sense of loss rises in me, no spirit to rally against fate, or the inevitability that I shall not reach my destination, my would-be home.

Home. It lies in memory and dream. I welcome either as I close my eyes, the jostling and rattling of the plane and the murmurs and nervous chattering of its passengers like a white-noise blanket swaddling the moments I seek to hold on to forever or at least until my end. Home is there beyond the veil, where Marco lives now. No matter where I go, home is always with me, so long as I carry his memory.

It must be better to die than to return to a place filled with unfamiliar faces and false pretenses, where distant relatives seek to curry favor, no doubt hoping I'd die soon and leave them the wealth Marco and I accumulated over a lifetime of hard work, of happiness earned. Yet feeling this, I still got on this plane.

I smooth out my slacks, hoping Marco's eyes light up when he sees me again like they always did. It has been so lonely without him these past several years. And if I close my eyes tightly, I can almost see his mischievous grin and those chocolate-brown eyes twinkling as he romances me. The smell of his cologne lingers in the cabin.

A squalling child rips me from my tranquility. *Soon, Marco. Soon.* The mirage was wonderful but not real, not yet. The American beside me is real, handsome in his own right but not my

Marco. The comparison is unfair, as love tends to turn faults and flaws into endearments. I have no love for this man next to me beyond that which I have for all living things, though I surely pity time cut short.

Yes, I have lived, and I welcome what comes after. I sense the American still has those worth living for. What can be done? God takes those on His schedule, whether they're ready or not. So I ignore his panic and close my eyes again, letting my breaths come in and out in a steady cadence and enveloping myself in the white noise of chaos. The smile warms my face, then Marco's smile, and I find peace again even as a metal bird screeches its torment through the night.

Marco's face blurs. The American's worn look replaces it along with his own brand of cologne, a mixture of sweat and fear laden with the bubbly carbonation of one who cannot let go.

I sigh. I cannot yet let go either, not while another suffers so beside me. *C'est la vie, mais c'est la guerre. Marco, I will see you again soon.*

The breath I release rasps over my lips. The American is staring at a closed shutter. The lightning is so close outside that it illuminates the cabin wall like a projector behind a movie screen. His fingertips are carving rivets into the ends of his armrests. He is not ready to die.

If I lacked compassion, I might find his efforts to will himself against a fate he is impotent to escape laughable. He is a man trying to stop a wave from breaking, the effort only tearing himself apart on the inside and the outside. There is bravery in his fight but also in acceptance, and the latter can bring peace. In whatever time we have left, I will help him find that peace if I am able.

I slide my arm over his when something bounces off my nose. Oxygen masks dangle in front of me and the American, who seems utterly oblivious to them. His whole body is wound like a music box gear cranked as far as it will go. He clings to his chair as if it is a lifesaver on stormy waters. *And why not?* The plane rises and dips as if on high seas, with the storm so loud that it sounds like the angels are bowling. At least that's how Marco would have described the thunder. Perhaps he's up there with them, getting a strike.

I reach over and gently slide the American's mask over his head. He snaps his gaze toward me. Something behind his eyes is frenetic and mad like the glower of a rabid dog. As comprehension pervades his troubled mind, his stare begins to soften. Crow's-feet appear at the corners of his eyes as he nods his appreciation. I see in him now, a good man grappling with his fear. I offer him a smile, put on my own mask, and lay my hand on his.

After a moment, he releases his grip on the armrest and takes my hand: the beginnings of acceptance. He is a stranger sharing with me an intimacy not even Marco could have shared, two souls united on a journey into the ever-after. Though I am not afraid, I am thankful for his company.

I close my eyes for the last time. The howling wind and the squealing metal are much harder to block out now. No amount of effort can make me oblivious to the torrents of air and debris barraging my face. I need not see the end but only await a new beginning. *Marco, I'm coming home.*

Something wallops the bottom of the plane hard enough to send jolts up my legs. The American's grip tightens around my fingers, aggravating the knotted bone, and I hold my breath. *This is it.*

Several more thuds follow, like those lowriders kids drive bottoming out over speed bumps, until a final, concussive *thump* sends my stomach into my chest, and a sickly vibration runs through all my joints, as if they all turned into whacked funny bones. The sound that follows reminds me of sledding over rocks as a child, only much louder and coming from everywhere. A bang, like aluminum trash-can lids cymbal-crashing centimeters from my ears, dulls all subsequent racket even as the plane begins to roll. Over and over again, I tumble like a rodent in a hamster ball kicked by a sadistic child. My seat belt barely keeps me against my seat, like a lap bar on a rickety roller coaster. Pain flares in my hip, and I cry out, though I can barely hear me.

Agony forces my eyes open. Porcupine-like quills shoot at my face, and I shield it with my arms. My hair whips about like a flag tearing from its pole. I check on the American, who appears to be struggling with his seat belt when something big and hard cracks him in the forehead. His head snaps back violently. His eyes close, and he no longer moves of his own volition. I close my eyes again and tuck my head between my legs, just like the airline's safety video told us to do—but not before catching a glimpse of the front of the plane, where I see only darkness and inhale the aroma of evergreens.

a knot within a knot

Our rolling slows then stops, gravity telling me we're right side up, but we continue to slide as the plane's rear fishtails. We rise then crash down so hard that my hip seems to crumble beneath the weight of my torso. As we skid, the earth roars below me, but the sound is as dull as a soft timpani roll over my burst eardrum. With another tremendous *clang* like that of a shovel finding rock, we stop. My momentum carries me into the American, who is either too dead or too unconscious to care.

I bounce off him and return to my seat, my head whiplashing back with a *crack*. For a moment, I fear I have broken something, but other than superficial pain, bruised muscles, and severely agitated arthritis—all of which will undoubtedly blossom into debilitating agony over the next few weeks, should I live to see them—I seem to be unharmed.

Moreover, the plane has stopped moving. I make the sign of the cross and kiss the crucifix I wear around my neck. I know God and Marco have protected me and am overwhelmed by a mixture of relief and grief as I realize today is not yet my time. Apparently, I have been given an edict. I have taken the American into my care, and I must see to him.

"Bless you, Marco."

The American sits slumped over, and I gently nudge him back against his seat. His chest rises and falls with even breaths, so I know he's alive, though I cannot assess the extent of his injuries.

I stick my finger into my ear in an attempt to unclog it. The wails coming from in front of me and behind me grow louder but still sound as if they're being transmitted through water. So many are hurt but still alive. To hear so much suffering, I almost wish I'd gone deaf.

At least those with voices still have a chance. From what I know of those black boxes planes are required to have, help should already be on the way. *Except . . . aren't those boxes kept in the front of the plane?*

I say a prayer for the missing then undo my seat belt so that I might help any present. As I start to rise, a debilitating pain makes me crumple back into my seat. I join the chorus of wails. My hips have always ached, mostly when going up stairs and sitting or standing for long intervals, but the hurt that shoots through my entire pelvis is far more than any flare-up I've previously experienced. It feels and trembles like jelly and will not support movement. It's broken. I'm sure of it. Like so many others, I am confined to my chair until help arrives.

If help arrives.

I wait, silently sobbing and failing to bite back my pain, for I don't know how long. With my hip shattered, every second is its own eternity. The torment is both blinding and mind-numbing, and my consciousness wavers.

A loud *creak* up ahead snaps me back into focus. I gasp as the front of the plane—or at least the front of the remaining tail end of the plane—rises several inches and hovers there. I crane my neck to peer over the seat in front of me. Moonlight pours in from no more than fifteen rows up, a shadowy form framed in its glow. A circle of light crowns a giant figure. I have died after all, and the angels have come to claim me. I straighten and narrow my gaze. *Maybe it's Marco.*

But no. This angel's eyes glint ruby red.

Those closer to the night air call for help, be it to the angel or because of it. Others scream. The plane crashes back down to a discord of cries and shrieks. Moonlight creeps deeper into the cabin, and the night goes silent. The cabin stills, as if every passenger has gone deer in the headlights, hoping to hide in plain sight from whatever lurks beyond the confines of their doomed vessel. The angel has abandoned us.

"Marco?" I don't feel him with me.

A melodic baritone voice that could only belong to a higher power resonates through the remnants of the plane, but the language it carries is entirely foreign to me. I guess maybe it's Latin, Gaelic, or some unique combination of the two.

Another sound replaces the voice—the snort of a Clydesdale or perhaps a large bear, for the sound is crisp and clear, loud enough to reach my ears over the din of the injured. Again, I peek over the seat, and my breath hitches. A thick tangle of branches crisscrossing one another like brambles or a dense mangrove barricades the way out. This alone is not alarming, but it appears to be drawing nearer. We must still be moving, drifting slowly into it. I don't know whether we're sliding, sinking, or what, but seeing the thicket coming closer, together with hearing that wild beast snort and the clomping of hooves, sends my heart trotting. The wails that come from what is now the front of the plane give way to panicked shouting and people scurrying over the backs of seats or fighting one another to reach the aisle. A middle-aged woman wearing a neck noodle races past, mascara running down her cheeks. I try to catch her to ask what's happening, but she has passed before I so much as raise a finger.

Gritting my teeth, I lean over the American and glance down the aisle. The pain in my hip is impossible to ignore, but I manage to hold the position long enough to see the woman disappear into a restroom, locking out a man trying to force his way in with her. Ahead, a passenger clearly too injured to move raises a fist over the aisle as the brambles swallow the row in which she sits. The arm jerks then falls limp.

And still, we slip toward the thicket. *No . . . the branches are moving toward us.*

Retreating to my seat, I cover my mouth as I hold back a scream. It's as if winter-dead trees are somehow alive and have taken offense to our plane's presence or perhaps seek to avenge the comrades it fell as it barraged over their landscape. Nearly reaching the cabin roof, the many-forked limbs are now visible over the chair in front of me. As impossible as I know it to be, I cannot deny what my eyes show me. The thicket continues forward, pushing row after row of seats with it, their bolts snapping and metal twisting as an ungodly force wrenches them from their natural positions. The chairs and those in them are crushed, mangled, and impaled against something that should, under any other circumstances, break against them.

With a heavy grunt, the brambles heave forward. Though most passengers struggle to flee the creeping death, they aren't as fortunate as the lady in the restroom or even the guy banging on its door. Many are too injured to attempt escape or too panicked to proceed rationally. Hands tremble as they rattle their seat belts and scream for help. Even the most agile and collected only manage to climb over a row or two of seats before their limbs become entangled with those of injured, frenzied passengers and pinned beneath the weight of the seats and the dead within them. The aisle is life, at least for a little while, and those who realize that claw, kick, and scrabble their way into it, piling on top of one another, crushing and stomping those on the bottom with no regard.

A few more passengers race past.

"Help!" I call, my voice barely more than a whisper. If they hear me, they ignore me.

I shake the American. "Wake up! Wake up!" Wincing, I shake him harder. "We need to move!"

He sleeps peacefully, blissfully ignorant of his impending death. If I can wake him, I know he would not leave me. But he will not awaken, and even the small motions I make in my attempts to rouse him drain my energy and resolve. "Wake up. Please wake up."

A sound so out of place amid the wailing and begging comes from somewhere at my feet: a child's giggle. I look down to see a little girl in pigtails crawling under the seats. I reach for her, but she scrambles under the seat in front of me as if she thinks we're playing tag. I lunge, inflaming my hip to eye-and-teeth-clenching levels, and grab her sneaker, but it slips off in my hand. Before I can reach for her foot, she is gone, heading toward her doom. "Wait! Come back, child!"

To be old and helpless when I'm most needed fills me with shame. To have died in the crash, quickly and without pain, might have been ideal and would certainly be better than this gruesome horror show. I have patiently awaited death, but I never imagined it would come so painfully or to so many others while I am forced to sit idly by. And that beast's snort, getting louder, drawing nearer, is ever present as the vast creature hides somewhere within those brambles.

I clench my fist and slam it onto the armrest. I've built a life from nothing, working hard every day until my bones grew too weary to keep going. But I'll be damned if I won't force them to work now. I undo my belt and push myself up on trembling legs. For all my mind's strength, the toll my body has taken is too much. I gasp in pain, shedding tears in waterfalls down my cheeks, and I fall back into my seat. Defeated. Dead.

After catching my breath, I whisper an apology to the American I could not save and to the little girl who slipped through my grasp.

Like a bulldozer trolling slowly forward, the branches bring promise of slow impalement. A grunt of exertion, almost human, comes from the thicket, now only six rows from me. The branches reach for the ceiling, fabric, gore, and viscera decorating them like garland around a Christmas tree. A massive head belonging to a stag three times as big as any I have ever seen supports the wicked tapestry. Its fur is midnight black, its eyes emerald green, and it would otherwise be beautiful and awe-inspiring if not for the human remains dripping down its heavy coat. Its neck, thick with muscle, as broad as a tree trunk, does not seem strained beneath the masses entwined in its multipronged antlers. The creature's girth widens the aisle as it steps forward, as if nothing blocks its path. The floor squeals under a hoof the size of a large frying pan.

A speared woman twitches against the ceiling, not yet dead. Luckier ones are very much so, while others no longer resemble the sum of their missing parts. *Scrape, scrape,* the antlers' sharp tips drag along the ceiling.

The little girl in pigtails peers over the seat in front of me. She giggles, apparently unaware of the hideous monster only a couple of meters away from her back. I sputter incoherently, trying to form the right words that would make her hide and keep her safe. I force a smile then draw my hands over my eyes. "*Un, deux, trois, quatre . . .* "

I hear a giggle and chance a peek. The little girl is gone, I hope understanding my intent to play hide and seek. *I'm sorry, child. I won't be able to come find you.*

I look to my left and shriek. The stag's head is maybe a dozen centimeters from the American's. It snorts again, warm, moist air shooting from its snout and making the hairs on my arms rise. A huge black tongue lolls from its mouth, slithers like a snake over the American's chair, then finds his face, lathering him with spit but washing away the blood.

My heart is pounding. I want to slap the beast away before it can hurt me or my unconscious travel companion. "Marco . . . please help me."

I think I see him then, my love, reflected in the giant beast's eyes. The animal releases another snort, and the odors of pine and musk emanate from its muzzle. Its head turns toward me, its giant nostrils expanding as it takes in my scent. I curl away, trying to melt into the seat, its hot breath tickling my neck. When it snorts again, I find my courage. I turn to face it and throw myself over the American, shielding his body. "No. You cannot have us, beast."

A melodic whistle comes from somewhere outside the plane. The stag rises and leans against the American's chair, over which my arm has been cast in a pathetic attempt to protect him. Its weight catches two of my fingers around his armrest, and I howl as they crack. But the beast pays me no attention as it shuffles backward, dragging chairs, bodies, and bits of ceiling with it.

I reach for the American's hand with my remaining good fingers as my chest tightens. The pressure amplifies, as if a powerlifter is squeezing my heart. Pain travels down my left arm and up my neck. My head spins, or maybe it's the plane. Anxiety heightens the pressure in my chest, which in turn heightens my anxiety. *Marco? Where is Marco?*

My eyelids flutter, and I try to focus. But I don't see Marco. *You're supposed to be here. Where are you?* Darkness comes over my eyes, and I think only of Marco and pray he is not one with the Beast.

summons

william meikle

nO LIMBS, NO LIMBS, *no head, no head, left arm gone, left leg gone, no legs, no head.*

The row of stick figures was carved with a degree of precision Dave knew he'd never be able to master but that didn't make them any less puzzling. They were etched into the old beams of his attic, aged in place as if they had been done at the time the roof space was built, but they hadn't been there two weeks ago, and there had been nobody else in the house for that same period but himself. They were an impossibility made possible by the fact that they were undeniably right there in front of him.

He hadn't been up here since the day he'd put his overflow boxes in situ when he moved in over a year ago, and he'd only come up to retrieve a box of vinyl having had an urge to listen to some early Pink Floyd. That quest was forgotten as soon as he switched on the single bulb and saw what had been carved, not just on the beam above the hatchway, but apparently on every available slat and strut of wood in the timber-framed area. They marched, a myriad of stick figures with limbs or heads or both missing, and Dave was still trying to figure out not just what they signified but how they got there in the first place.

Maybe the bulb is going. Maybe they were always there and it's only because of dimmer light and shifting shadows that I see them now.

He was trying to manufacture a rational explanation but he'd been up here too long now to be able to blithely explain away this manifestation as a trick of the light; the figures still marched no matter which way he looked at them. It was a new thing in his life and he wasn't sure he wanted to welcome it. There had been far too many new things in his life these past months; one more might be the straw that broke the camel's back to send him spiralling, for despite his fear of the new, his despair at the old wasn't anything he relished revisiting.

He decided to stop trying to deny the evidence of his eyes and take a closer look.

*No left leg, no head, no limbs, no right arm, no arms, no head
and no legs.*

The figures were arranged in tiny ranks, each an inch high, half
an inch wide and all spaced exactly the same distance apart on
either side and on top and bottom with almost military precision
. . . a little marching army. An impossible little marching army. It
was a work of great craftsmanship while simultaneously being
completely baffling. It made Dave's eyes swim just to look at it and
the more he looked at it the dizzier he became, all too aware of his
heartbeat pounding. He beat a hasty retreat downstairs when he
started to hyperventilate.

Two minutes later he was in the front room nursing a glass of
Scotch he didn't remember pouring, listening to a pounding in his
ears, hoping he wasn't as close to a heart attack as he felt. He
looked over to the mantelpiece.

"What do you reckon, Anne? Is your auld man finally going
doolally?"

Anne didn't reply; she hadn't replied for a year now but Dave
kept talking to her anyway, kept hoping. If he could just hear her,
just once, everything might make a bit more sense. But she was
still silent, so unlike herself.

Dave had never harboured any illusions about any kind of
afterlife; he'd been raised Scottish Protestant, church and Sunday
School, R.E. at the comprehensive, but none of it had taken. He
had remained a pragmatist all his adult life. But that didn't mean
he couldn't hope. He'd been hoping these past twelve months.

He remembered the day every time his gaze fell on the urn on
the shelf above the grate.

It was a Saturday.

She'd gone on the preceding Thursday.

"Just a quick bit of business," she'd said. "I'll be back before
you know it."

He'd busied himself in books, she'd gone to get her plane. He
hadn't listened to the radio or watched TV so didn't know there had
been a crash until he got what he afterwards always thought about
as *'the phone call'*, always hearing it in italics in his head. The only
thing he remembered for a while were small words . . . died,
instantly, no pain. Tears, grief, cremation and more grief followed,
then, after a few months, she'd come with him in the urn, out of the
city to this house on the coast for a quiet retirement by the sea.

And quiet it had been. Dave spent his days walking the cliff paths and sitting on his porch watching the ever changing moods of the North Sea. Every Wednesday he'd wander up to Finsburgh for a trip to the local library and a couple of pints with lunch in the pub in the harbour. At night he read, watched old movies and sipped old whisky. Sometimes, like now, he'd talk to Anne and hoped. It helped.

That was Dave's life now, one of quiet days and lonely nights, a well spent life now cast adrift from its moorings, slowly winding down.

But now there was this.

No left leg, no head, no limbs, no right arm, no arms, no head and no legs.

He couldn't get them out of his head. He finished off the whisky and went back up to the attic. The figures were, impossibly, still there, still looking as if they'd been there as long as the house had stood. He considered turning his back, closing the hatch and ignoring them but he knew that would only lead to more preying on his mind. Better to confront them directly. He went downstairs, retrieved his laptop, and returned with it to start transcribing the phenomena.

It didn't take him long to get small graphics set up for each of the figures, then it became a matter of methodically cutting and pasting them in order into a document. He picked a random starting point on the first beam above the hatchway and set to it. He was soon lost in the routine of it, falling into a cutting-and-pasting rhythm that was almost soothing.

By the time he went to bed that first night he'd managed to copy down two struts' worth of figures, less than a twentieth of the whole thing by his estimate. He went to sleep with marching men flitting across his mental landscape and a pounding drum of a headache.

He dreamed he was someone else.

Marcus Caelius got his first look at his destination when they crested a hill and finally descended out of the damp, dismal fog that had been their constant companion for the last two days. It was autumn of the year 1133 Ab urbe condita and the thing most preying on the general's mind was the Edict of Thessalonica. He'd received word from Rome that Theodosius I, with co-emperors Gratian and Valentinian II, had declared their wish that all Roman citizens convert to trinitarian Christianity. Caelius's men weren't ready for that. Caelius definitely wasn't ready; he had enough mystery in his life without adding more. He forced his mind away; he wouldn't need to make a decision until he returned to Rome, and he wasn't intending to make that trip for many years yet, if ever. He looked to the road in front of him.

The rough fort of Rumabo ahead of them did not look any more inviting than the country they had been passing through and he wished that he could have stayed, snug and nearly warm, in his country quarters south of the wall of Hadrian. But Flavius Butto, the officer in command here, had asked for him specifically, calling on a family favour, and Caelius could not ignore the request without losing face. Besides, the cohort was in trouble. As an army man of long standing he was duty-bound to render any aid he could.

Once, he too had commanded a cohort, leading them in battles ranging across the wilds of Germania. But now here he was, at the most northern, most western outpost of the Empire, with only five men at his side. They had ridden for four days in relentless damp and drizzle through moor and bog, and now they were looking down over the Antonine Wall.

On first impressions the wall was a great disappointment. Second impressions did not make it any less so. In truth, it was little more than a large ditch with delusions of grandeur, nothing like the massive, whitewashed stone edifice with which Hadrian had stamped his legacy across the country to the south. Here, a hundred miles further north, the weather was that much more inclement, the natives that much more savage and the country that much more unforgiving of invaders. All of which served to make wall building that much more impractical.

The earthworks were at least large and impressive, with small forts every two miles and a wooden track atop the whole length so that it could be patrolled. But given the openness of its aspect, patrols were, of necessity, frequent, and the manpower required to keep the wall secure was vastly disproportionate to its strategic importance. Caelius had known all of this before he left home, but seeing it for himself only reinforced his long held belief.

We should not be here.

It seemed he was not the only one with such thoughts, for Butto's message had been short and to the point.

"In the name of the debt that you owe my father, I beseech you—come quickly. Something is killing my men."

Butto himself stood by the fort's gatehouse as they approached, as if he had been watching for their arrival. The commander was some twenty years younger, but Cailius would have known him anywhere; he had his father's features, features Caelius had last seen on a bloody field on the edge of a forest, where the father of the man before him had taken a spear meant for Caelius himself, and subsequently died in agony of the sepsis. It looked like the younger man had suffered similar agonies; strain was etched around his eyes and mouth and when he spoke it was with the relief of a man who suddenly thought himself freed of a great burden.

Caelius got the story over a flagon of hot wine by the fireside in Butto's quarters while he tried, not quite successfully, to get some warmth back into his bones after his journey.

"I am retired, Butto," he said. "You know that. I have no jurisdiction here. I am only here because of the service I owe you."

Butto looked tired, as if he had not slept in many days.

"It is not your jurisdiction I require," the younger man said. "But your strength—and your knowledge. I know you have made a study of the Elder cults."

Of all the things that Caelius had imagined he would hear on his arrival, this was the least expected.

"In Rome, yes, and as a much younger man—but they have no bearing here."

"Do not be so sure, Caelius," Butto said. "We are far from Rome—far from civilised places altogether, as I have all too much cause to ponder."

It took some coaxing, but finally Caelius persuaded Butto to sit with him at the fire and, slowly, over several more flagons of wine, the story finally got told.

"My men are a superstitious lot," Butto began. "The Sixth Cohort of Nervii are Belgae and Gallic recruits and before we civilised them they were as equally savage as the Celts we fight here, and equally as pagan. I did not have much trouble with them while we were garrisoned in some almost genteel farmlands near Londinium, but moving them north to patrol this wall has only brought to the fore old beliefs that Rome should have knocked out of them in training.

"It started well enough, back in the spring. I should have noted there was something amiss when the previous commander of the wall seemed a little too keen to be departing, but in truth I was proud of my new command and the trust Rome was showing in me, a trust I promised myself to live up to.

It was just as wet then as it is now, but at least it was a little warmer. The men did their duty, any raids from the north were summarily dealt with, and discipline was easily maintained. But it was not long before I started to hear stories—of music being heard in the night, and of a fog where there should be no fog. I put it down to the men's aforesaid superstitions—perhaps if I had paid more heed back then things might be different now—but as I have said, I was new to the post, keen to make my mark on it, and hard on the men as a result.

"The first man died three weeks ago and more stories quickly followed—more stories of music and fog. After the second man died I almost had a rebellion on my hands, and the men refused to patrol alone, so I instigated pairs, then fours.

"Another man died, then another. That is when I sent for you, Caelius. I know of your area of expertise."

"I do not think I can help much. You have a Celt problem, that much is certain. They are getting past your defences somehow."

"No, Caelius—you do not understand. Each man that has died has not a mark on him—no wounds, and no poison, for I have had them tested. They have all fallen at their posts, heart-struck— heart-struck and terrified out of their wits."

"I still say it must be the Celts," Caelius replied.

"Even if I tell you I have seen the fog, and heard the music for myself?" Butto said softly. "Even then?"

Caelius went quiet.

"And since you wrote to me? Have things changed?"

"It still comes—we lose a man—sometimes two—every night, and I have had three more deserters just today. At this rate we'll be done for by the first day of winter."

"They are all taken on patrol?"

Butto nodded.

"And all on the same stretch of wall."

Caelius groaned, and stretched.

"You had better show me."

Caelius took a heavy cloak when it was offered—it was sheepskin, lined with coarse, matted wool. It smelled rank, but it was warm, and mostly kept the damp out, so it was most welcome when they ventured out on the ramp above the earthworks, especially so when their vigil stretched into its second hour.

There was nothing to be seen out in the lands to the north, just unbroken moorland, dank pools and wispy mist. Tiny biting insects plagued them constantly—they came in swarms as thick as smoke at times, such that Caelius took to huddling deep inside the cloak with only his nose showing.

Butto's man—an Egyptian slave—stood behind them carrying a deerskin of warm wine from which they partook at intervals. What with that, the heat inside the sheepskin, and the seeping tiredness from his long journey to get here, Caelius was starting to feel drowsy as night fell.

He forced himself to attention as soon as he noted his head drooping. An old soldier knows well how to give the appearance of being on guard while catching what little rest there was to be found, and he wasn't that far gone into age and softness that he had forgotten his own days on patrols such as these. Butto had been speaking, and he'd missed some conversation, but before Caelius could form a polite reply, he heard a noise in the air. It wasn't coming from beyond the wall—it wasn't coming from anywhere in particular, it was just there—everywhere at once—a high, off-key flute, playing a tune he thought he should recognize, but could not.

Butto's eyes went wide, the whiteness showing starkly in the gathering gloom. His man, the Egyptian, took a step backward, as if intending to flee, but Caelius put a stop to that with a sharp glance. The flute playing got louder still, and a fog rose up, seeming to seep upward from the earthworks itself.

The sound of the flute filled the whole length of the walkway, piping high and whining. Caelius' sight was filled with shimmering, dancing points of static. The walkway, fort, ditch and his companions seemed to melt away, falling into white motes. A black cavernous well formed in front of him, receding away, impossibly deep, impossibly distant. The Egyptian gave out a yell, then a wail as high as the flute itself. Something danced and cavorted as it fell into the blackness, falling ever faster away from Caelius, growing taller, thinner—far, far too thin—as the dark well took it. Caelius realised he was seeing the very essence of what made the Egyptian man be taken from him—an essence that danced and stretched away to where the flautist piped it home—thin—like a matchstick—as it fell into the vastness of eternity.

When Caelius recovered his senses, the night was quiet, there was no fog, and Butto stood over the dead Egyptian at their feet. The man looked like he had died in abject terror.

"Quickly," Caelius said when Butto showed no sign of moving. "Get him inside—we cannot let your men see that another has fallen while we stood beside him."

Between them they carried the slave along the walkway, and got his body into Butto's chambers where they rolled it in a rug and hid it in a dark corner.

"We shall have to dispose of him quietly in the morning," Caelius said.

Butto nodded.

"I have another man I can trust to do the job. But why are we still here? Why did it take him and not either of us? Surely we are the bigger prize?"

Caelius shucked off his cloak then lifted the wineskin from where they'd left it when they came in, and headed for the fire. He didn't answer Butto's question until they were both sitting by the fireside with flagons filled.

"I do not think it is a matter of prizes, my friend," he said. "I have felt its like before—it takes who it can—whoever succumbs to it most willingly."

"So it can be fought?"

"Yes—with heart and will and all the strength you can muster—as it is with any battle."

"And you say you know what it is?"

"No—I said I have met its like before—but that is a tale for the morning. For now, I will finish this wine, and I will sleep. Ask me no more until then."

Dave woke, confused as to where he was, who he was, but thin morning light coming through the patterned curtains quickly rooted him back in reality and the strange dream quickly faded until it was barely remembered even as he rolled out of bed.

After a quick breakfast he was right back in the attic with the stick figures. He tried to be meticulous, to ensure no faults in his transcription, but after a while the rows swam and merged and the drumbeat in his head got too large to allow concentration. He retreated downstairs, made a pot of coffee and took his laptop out to the porch to look over what he'd done already.

Despite having spent the morning at it the figures still baffled him as much as ever. There seemed to be no rhyme nor reason to them.

No left leg, no head, no limbs, no right arm, no arms, no head and no legs.

At least the coffee dispelled the headache to no more than a dull throb but now that he was out in the fresh air he felt no compulsion to return to the attic. He fetched a jacket and went out onto the cliff path.

As always the breeze of the sea, the wish and wash of waves on pebbled shore and the cries of kittiwakes did much to centre him. But as soon as he got home and his gaze fell on the laptop screen the small drumbeat began again. Five minutes later he was back in the attic, back transcribing, lost in the marching rows of figures.

The sun was most of the way down in the west when he emerged out of an almost trance-like state. A check of his laptop told him he'd transcribed twenty pages of figures but he had little memory of doing it. The whole thing had become automatic, almost ritualistic. He had no idea whether he'd made any mistakes and his headache was such that he was past caring.

He retreated downstairs, substituted whisky for coffee and stared out to sea waiting for the pounding to subside. Every time he closed his eyes he saw the figures marching there. Those in the attic yet to be transcribed called out to their brothers; Dave felt it, like an almost physical tug at his mind, imploring him to return to them. He used the whisky to fight off the urge and spent the night eating pizza and drinking. Normally he'd have an old movie on, one of Anne's favourites, but tonight there was only the laptop screen and the figures. When the whisky took hold and they actually did appear to march he knew it was time for bed.

As soon as his head hit the pillow, darkness called for him and he dived gratefully into it.

He dreamed again, of a time long past and yet somehow right here beside him.

Caelius slept for almost twelve hours, a combination of the effects of the wine, his journey and the events of the night before. The body of the Egyptian—and the rug—were both gone when he rose in the late morning. Butto was on a tour of inspection of the men and the fort, so he had time for himself in which to think, but his mind was fogged and muddled. He felt more like himself after a bath and a light breakfast, during which he pondered the manner of the thing he'd seen on the walkway. Then, unable to put it off any longer, he went to ask his God for advice.

As an old soldier, he had long followed Mithras, and, as he knew there would be, the fort had a temple, deep in its foundations. What he had not expected was that the temple would be housed inside an obviously much older cavern. The walls were built of large blocks of sandstone, beautifully engineered and dovetailed together so tight that a layer of silk could not have been slid between them. During the long years of his own hunt for the Great Mystery, Caelius had visited several of these old tombs, in Carnac in France, on Malta and on the rolling moors in the South of this island. This chamber gave the same sense of age as any other he had visited, a remnant of a time long past and a reminder of the impermanence of all things.

What was completely different here though was the overwhelming sense that this place was still occupied by something much older than any Roman—he felt it, in every rustle, in every breath of wind, in every shift of shadow.

The statue of Mithras was in an alcove that was only a small part of a rough-hewn chamber of some antiquity. As his eyesight adjusted to the gloom he saw that the walls were covered in small carvings. At first Caelius thought it might be a language, but it was none that he recognised from his studies, indeed, it seemed to bear no resemblance to anything he had ever seen before. Whoever had drawn the figures had packed them tightly, a miniature army ranked side by side in tightly regimented formation. Some had all four limbs, some were missing an arm or a leg, and some were just a single streak with a dot for the head. It did not take him long to realise that he was not actually looking at crude representations of men at all—it was a code—perhaps even a language, albeit one with which he was completely unfamiliar.

He whistled. Something beneath whistled back, the same high flute he had heard on the walkway. Then came the first indication that there was more to this than a mere spectral flautist. A tear in space appeared in the centre of the chamber, blacker still than any shadow. It floated at his eye level and spun slowly in a clockwise direction. As he watched, it changed shape, settling into a new configuration, a black, somewhat oily in appearance droplet little more than an inch across at the thickest point. It seemed to be held in mid-air by some strange force.

And it looked most like an egg.

Caelius drew his knife from its sheath; it might not provide him any protection but its presence in his hand reassured him and fortified his resolve not to flee. As he stepped forward a rainbow aura thickened around the hanging egg, casting the whole chamber in dancing washes of soft colours as it continued to spin. The knife in his hand hummed and vibrated as he moved closer. The egg quivered and pulsed. And now it seemed larger than before. The chamber started to throb, like a heartbeat. The egg pulsed in time. And now it was more than obvious—it was most definitely growing. The knife sent a new flash of heat, like a searing burn in his palm as he lifted the weapon, but before he could strike the egg, the throb became a rapid thumping; the chamber shook and trembled. The vibration rattled his teeth and set his guts roiling. A blinding flare of blue light blasted all coherent thought from his head.

When he recovered enough to look back there was nothing to be seen hanging there but empty space. The black egg was gone as quickly as it had come and the chamber was once again dark and quiet.

He walked up out of the chamber, measuring his steps until he reached the fort, then retraced his steps up on the walkway in the same number of paces. He was standing right where they had been the night before—and he now knew that the spot was directly above the ancient carved chamber.

Caelius also now knew what he was dealing with—and now he was worried.

In the morning Dave's compulsion had gone. Despite the whisky he felt alert and clear headed. After coffee on the porch he took the laptop up to the attic, intending to finish what he'd started.

The figures were gone. All the beams and struts were smooth and no matter how he moved the light and shadows there was no sign they had ever existed, the smooth wood seeming to mock him at every attempt. The only proof of their existence he had was the document on his laptop.

And that's no kind of proof at all.

During the course of the day he must have opened and closed the document a dozen times, just to confirm the existence of the marching figures, worried every time that he'd be met with only a blank page, evidence of his own delusions.

He might have taken to the whisky early if he hadn't glanced at Anne's ashes on the mantel; that was enough. Even a hint of her disapproval kept the bottle in the cupboard. Instead he tried to rectify his slackness of the day before and cooked a proper meal; trout, new potatoes and peas, washed down with water and coffee. By the time evening came round the events of the previous forty-eight hours were taking on the shadow and soft textures of a dream, merging with his half-formed memories of the dreams of a Roman fort into a confused tangle, a mystery that refused to give him any clue as to how to unlock its secrets. He closed the laptop with no further thought for it, put on a favourite movie and settled back to wallow in instant nostalgia. General Sternwood was about to explain the McGuffin to Marlowe.

"You're looking, sir, at a very dull survival of a very gaudy life, crippled, paralyzed in both legs, I barely eat and my sleep is so near waking it's hardly worth a name. I seem to exist largely on heat, like a newborn spider."

A whisper ran in Dave's head.

No legs.

He pushed the thought away and lost himself in the movie. As it had been doing for decades, it sucked him in completely and he was soon taken away in the snap and snarl of the dialogue until one particular line jolted him upright in his seat as if hit by an electric shock.

"What you see is nothing. I've got a Balinese dancing girl tattooed across my chest."

He had no idea why but the movie had suddenly lost its charm, as if a switch had been pulled. Bogie was still giving it his all but Dave had stopped noticing. Once again the whisky called to him and this time he answered. He switched off the movie, poured a stiff one and took it out to the porch bench to watch moonlight dance on the sea and glint on the turning vanes of the wind farm on the horizon.

Tiredness, whisky and familiarity did their jobs. His eyes drooped, the Scotch forgotten. At some point he fell asleep.

When he woke it was morning and there was a stranger sitting next to him on his bench. Dave wasn't unduly alarmed; given the house's position on the cliff path he often had ramblers stop by for a chat. They didn't generally come up onto the porch uninvited, but this old chap looked like he'd needed a rest. It was hard to tell as he was sitting down, but he couldn't have been more than five feet tall, and wizened with it, with a face like cracked leather, hands as fragile as old dry paper, and a wispy grey beard stained yellow at the lips with nicotine. His eyes were the youngest part of him, a piercing blue that matched the shimmering sea below the cliff. When he spoke it was with a rumble, as if something was broken in his chest.

"I have been sitting here watching the sun rise and considering the metaphors in those windmills out there. As I have watched these shores all these years, so shall these wonders of science watch, drawing their circles in the sky in much the same way that I began, with my circles on paper," the man said without preamble. He was old and unnaturally thin but his voice was strong.

He turned and took Dave's right hand in his.

"I have a story to tell you, if you'll listen?"

Dave smiled.

"Let me fetch a pot of coffee for us. Then, my morning's free and you can tell me anything you like."

When Dave returned ten minutes later he half expected the old man to be gone, faded like his dreams, but he was still there in the same place, and took to the coffee with some gusto before he started to speak. Dave was soon lost in his story.

I was late in arriving in Fortingall having missed a connection in Perth so it was near midnight by the time the coachman dropped me at the doorstep of the kirk. Then there was only time to reacquaint myself with my old friend John, partake of several large glasses of his fine Scotch and wend a weary way to bed.

So it was that my first sight of the old tree came in the flush of morning with a mist on the ground and a stiff breeze in my face. John had told me about the yew in his letters of course but there had been nothing that could have prepared me for the sense of history that the sight of it brought. It is an aged thing indeed, its original core having been long since hollowed out by time and weather, leaving a myriad of secondary branches gathered around the remains of a gnarled old trunk that looks more like stone than wood. John joined me for a pre-breakfast smoke as I circled the trunk below the canopy, feeling my way around the thing.

"I knew you would like it," he said. "I have it on good authority from a professor of Botany at the University that it predates Christ himself. Just think of what memories of Christmas past it could show us if we could only unfold them."

"I thought they placed yews in churchyards, not the other way around," I said, laughing.

"For all we know this old tree here is where they got the idea," John replied, and I almost laughed again before I saw that he was being serious.

I did not get a chance to follow up on it for just then his housekeeper called us in for breakfast and I was treated to a mound of eggs, ham and toast that took three pots of strong tea to wash down and all I was fit for during the rest of the morning was sitting in an armchair in John's study while we caught up with our friendship.

It had been several years since our last meeting. They had been quiet ones for him here in his wee kirk in rural Perthshire, rather less quiet for me in the Transvaal with the regiment. Now here I was home, furloughed, lamed and looking in the face at the prospect of a bleak retirement. That tale of the change in my circumstances is too long and far too dull to relate here. Suffice to say my friend John listened as a friend should and his reply was not to scold or berate me for my depression but to fetch out the smokes.

Once I was feeling more like myself again I turned conversation from my personal woes around to the business of the yew tree. It quickly became clear that John had been putting his quiet time to good use for he had a treasury of knowledge of the tree's history at his command. He treated me to what he had learned and also much of what he suspected. It was fascinating stuff indeed, but little of it is germane to my story here except for what he said at the last.

"You know, there's even a story that Pontius Pilate himself sat under this very tree as a boy when his father governed this part of the country for Rome. And later the Antonine wall passed, almost through this very spot."

I had to laugh at that.

"It's Christmas, old boy, not Easter."

He didn't rise to the bait and I saw that he had something on his mind.

"Okay, out with it," I said. "You didn't ask me up here for the weather. What's up?"

Before he answered he took two sheets of crumpled paper from his pocket and smoothed them out on the table.

"I have indeed got a story. But first, what do you make of that?"

I got up, rather reluctantly, and examined the paper. Both pieces had obviously been taken as rubbings, not from brass or stone but from wood. They showed what appeared to be a series of stick figures, most of whom were missing some part of their anatomy, no legs, or one leg but no head, that kind of thing. The figures covered the pages, twenty five lines to each, eight to a line, four hundred little men marching for a reason I could not even begin to fathom.

"It's Sherlock Holmes you need, not me old man," I said. "It's some kind of code, isn't it?"

"I think so. Although it is a peculiar one that has defeated me for a year to the very day. Are you ready for a snifter? I know it's not even noon, but it is Christmas after all."

I wasn't about to argue and minutes later we were settled by the fire again with fresh smokes lit and glasses filled as he sat with the papers in his lap.

"As I said, it was a year ago today," he started. "I went out to watch the sunset and by pure chance happened to be lined up with the tree between me and the last rays of the dying day. I saw, at the base of the oldest part of the trunk, what I took to be ridges hacked into the wood by a blade. At first I thought little of it then I noted their regularity and how they were tightly concentrated in a small space; it was something that had been done with a purpose in mind. The light was going from the sky quickly and somehow I knew I might not get another chance, so I ran indoors, giving my housekeeper a bit of a fright in the process, and came back to make these rubbings.

"Many a night between then and now I have sat here trying to penetrate the secret. And many nights I have gone out to stand by the tree at sunset but—and you will have to believe me on this—I have never again been able to find the little soldiers. It is as if they were only there for that particular minute, existing only for that single spot in time."

He went quiet then, both of us supping at our drinks and puffing smoke until I broke the silence.

"It is a mystery, to be sure," I replied, "but hardly one to get yourself worked up over, old boy. The old world is full of such mysteries; stones lined up with the solstices, menhirs used as calendars, that sort of guff. Surely this is just more of the same? The marks on the tree are still there, of course they are. They must be. It's just that they need the right light for them to show up."

"My thoughts exactly, or they were, last winter. But as the nights, and the sunsets went on and the marks never again revealed themselves I took to running my fingers over the wood, attempting to trace them by feel. I assure you, they are not there. Maybe they never were. And if you do not believe me, go look for yourself. You'll only find obdurate old wood, as I have done these many months."

I saw, too late, that the poor chap had gotten himself quite worked up. He'd invited me here hoping for some understanding, perhaps a sympathetic ear, and here I was offering him scepticism instead of friendship. I felt quite ashamed of myself. There and then I undertook to do something about it.

He had taken quite the huff with me and did not look up from the fireside as I took my leave and went once more out onto the kirk yard. I took more time with the old thing this time, sitting on my haunches close to the base of the trunk and running my hands over and around the aged bark, trying in vain to find the gouges that had shown up in the rubbings. I had a moment when I thought bad thoughts of my old friend, wondering whether this whole thing might be some fine Christmas prank of his. Then I remembered how he'd taken such a huff and I redoubled my efforts.

I must have been at it for a good twenty minutes and was no closer to feeling anything but cold bark when the strangest sensation came over me. It started in my fingertips, a buzzing vibration passing from the old tree through to my hands, my wrists, up my arms and into my head where a distant drumbeat started up, a martial rhythm that reminded me of nothing less than facing down the Zulu in the veldt. It quite discombobulated me and sent me back inside seeking sanctuary in the warmth of both the fire and a new glass of scotch in my belly.

By the time the housekeeper called us through to lunch John had quite forgiven me my earlier transgression. Over a fine meal of salmon, potatoes and greens, washed down by strong Scottish ale, we reaffirmed the joy of our long friendship and I made a promise to him to stand beside him at sunset. The vibration in my head had faded with the ale but I was no longer quite so sure that there would be nothing to see come the evening.

We spent the afternoon by the fireside again, sipping scotch and trying to make head or tail of the blasted marching stick figures but for the life of me I could see no pattern to the thing no matter how much I squinted at it.

"I've looked at it every bloody way I can think of," John said on seeing my exasperation. "I even showed it to a mathematician—David McLeish, you'll remember him from Edinburgh back in the day—he had the pages for two weeks in the summer but I brought them home none the wiser on their return. If it is indeed a code it's a damned devilish one."

"Have you had any thoughts at all as to why it might have been carved in the tree? Or when?"

"Thoughts, opinions, yes. But nothing in the way of hard facts. I can tell you that judging by the position of the carvings and the state of the bark that I believe the marks to have been made at least as far back as the Roman era."

"Don't give me that Pilate tale again," I pleaded. "My incredulity will only stretch so far."

That at least got me a laugh and another glimpse of the old friend I remembered. Our companionship sustained us through the afternoon in tales and anecdotes of our time as students in Auld Reekie and, after a few more scotches I found myself telling tales I had told no one else, of that last battle, of blood and thunder and Zulu songs and a leg wound that will pain me on damp nights for however long I have remaining. John had always had a sympathetic ear and today proved to be no different. I talked for hours while he kept our glasses filled and smokes coming. When it was done I felt hollowed out and empty but strangely more like myself than I had at any time since leaving Africa. When the housekeeper called us to the dining room for tea I even began to feel a long forgotten boyhood excitement for the forthcoming Christmas.

After a most pleasant tea John had us out in the Kirk yard again in time for the sunset but any hope of a ray of light on the matter was dashed by one of those particularly Scottish shifting mists that obscured everything beyond ten paces from the doorstep.

We stood there until the light went out of the sky completely and I could see by the slump of his shoulders that the disappointment was hitting my friend hard. I attempted to bring back the Christmas spirit by offering an early present, a Meerschaum pipe I had brought out of Africa for this very purpose. It did indeed bring a small smile to John's face but it wasn't long before he was back to sitting in front of the fire worrying at the two pieces of paper again.

"Look, John," I said. "It's Christmas. Don't you have any duties to your flock that you should be about?"

"The flock is widespread at the best of times," he said. "We used to have a midnight service on this night but after old Mrs McKenzie died that was the end of it, for I would only be speaking to an empty kirk. Now all I do is ring the bells to see in the day. If we stay sober long enough you can give me a hand with that later."

He was showing a distinct lack of enthusiasm, I must say. I attempted to bring him some cheer with some old soldier's stories, of battles fought, of rollicking drinking binges in the fleshpots and of comrades found and all too soon lost. He listened, as I have said, he has always listened but he still had the two sheaves of paper on his lap and every so often his eyes would drop to peruse the marching figures that so vexed him.

Staying sober proved to be beyond me under the circumstances. I'm afraid to say that I took to his Scotch with rather too much gusto. By the time it came round to almost midnight my head spun like a top and getting out of the armchair was almost beyond me.

"Stay where you are, old chap," John said. "I'll ring the bells and come back for a last snifter before bed."

Duty, to my friend and my conscience in the morning, forced me to stand and follow him through the manse and out to the belfry of the old kirk.

We had to pass the yew on the way and once again I felt the strangest vibration thrum through me, this time coming up out of the ground through the soles of my boots and upward via ankles, knees, thighs and hips into the barrel of my chest where it got my old heart beating in time.

John turned and held his oil lantern up to see my face.

"Are you all right? Are you sure you wouldn't be better back by the fire? Come, I'll see you back."

Even as he spoke the vibration faded, gone as quickly as it had come. I managed a smile I wasn't sure I had in me.

"Nonsense. Just a touch of the whisky vapours; it's not the first time you've seen me under their influence. Lay on MacDuff and don't spare the horses. Can't have Christmas without the bells, can we?"

When we arrived in the belfry John seemed much more like himself, the act of preparing the ropes and setting them up appearing to ground him back in the little joys that help to build reality. As for myself, I was happy to stand back and let him get on with it; the whisky had me feeling delicate and it wouldn't do to have anything come back up that should be staying down. Besides, John had it all well in hand. He checked his watch and smiled.

"Merry Christmas, old friend," he said, and pulled on the first cord. The peal of the bell rang loudly, echoing through the belfry. I felt it move my guts about then the second bell kicked in, the vibration rose and rose again to a pounding that set my heart to beating in time. A blaze of pure white noise blasted through me as if I'd stood too close to a cannon going off and for a while I knew nothing but darkness and the beat of the great drum.

"Facing down Zulu in the veldt?" Dave said. "Are you trying to tell me you fought in the Zulu wars? That's impossible."

"And yet, here I am, in all my glory. I think you know at least some of where this is coming from, and even where it might be going," the old man said. "I am not what I seem. Then again, who is?"

He smiled sadly then took a small leather bound book from his pocket. He opened it and showed Dave an illuminated diagram done in red, black and gold in a precision worthy of Dürer.

It was titled *MALAGMA*, and showed a fiery red serpent eating the world which was depicted as a shining golden disc.

"Strictly speaking," he said. "This isn't part of the process at all, rather, this is a symbolic representation of the whole. *Malagma* is Latin, meaning *Amalgamation*. The whole process, the quest if you like, is to amalgamate the soul, the *microcosm*, with the universe, the *macrocosm*."

"Sorry," Dave said, trying a smile. "You've lost me. Is there a point to this?"

The old man laughed.

"There's always a point. But I'm sorry to have confused you. Fourteenth century symbolism was obscure even then."

He went quiet for a short while before continuing.

"Do you know anything about Zen?"

It was Dave's turn to laugh.

"Only from reruns of *Kung Fu*."

"Well, Grasshopper, everything is one, and one is everything."

"*I am he as you are he as you are me and we are all together?*" Dave said.

"Yes," the old man replied. "We are the egg men. All together in one huge womb that is the Universe, the *macrocosm*. Alchemists were convinced that mercury transcended both states, both above and below, both life and death. It came to symbolise the transformation required to reach illumination and eternal life."

"Illumination?"

"Let's not get ahead of ourselves. I just wanted you to get some idea what we're getting into here."

"I wasn't aware I was getting into anything," Dave said. "I thought we were just passing the time of day."

"And passing it is. There is more to my tale, if you wish to hear it?"

"I think I had better, don't you?"

"Yes, for I can hear the Dreaming God's song call to me. You have kept a doorway open, whether by intention or accident it matters not, that I will soon have to pass through. It will not be long now."

Without further explanation, he began to speak again.

I came to myself in the kirk yard just as the mist lifted away and a full moon bathed the old tree in dancing shards of silver and grey.

"Look," John said in a hoarse whisper. "There."

My gaze followed his stare. There, etched in black against the trunk, proud in the moonlight, were the lines of stick figures..

No arms, head and left arm missing, no legs, no limbs, head and left arm missing, no legs, no legs, no legs.

Somewhere in the distance the drums continued to beat and were joined by a wailing as of a choir, far off in a strong wind. We were lost in a lament for the dead. A shadow play took place in front of my gaze as if projected against the last of the mist; a silent battle of dancers in the beat. Swords flashed, bodies fell.

No legs, no left arm, no head, no arms, one left leg, one right leg, just a torso, no head.

The drums pounded in my head like cannons going off, a multitude of voices rose to join the beat, a language I did not know but whose words came to me anyway there in the dance.

They dance in the deep with the worms in the dark
They dream with the earth in the depths
They dance and they sing with the gods in their sleep
And the Dreaming Gods are singing where they lie.

The dancing shadows fell apart into dust and light and moonbeams seeping onto the tree like water into a sponge.

Where they lie, where they lie, where they lie, where they lie
The Dreaming Gods are singing where they lie.

The drumbeat faded slowly, draining away somewhere far below us beneath the tree.

"In the deep, in the dark," John whispered, and just like that all was quiet, the moon went behind a cloud and there was only the kirk yard and the night and we two friends staring at each other in wonderment.

"What in blazes was that all about?" John said five minutes later as we made determined inroads into the last of the scotch by his fireplace.

"You don't see it, do you?" I replied. "I suppose it's because I'm a soldier that I do. At some point in distant history your tree saw a battle; I'm guessing it was your Romans against the locals, and the locals did not come out well in the fight. Afterwards, they set down their record; these days we carve our memorials in stone but they did it on the oldest thing they knew. They set the record of their dead in the tree, for them to remember, for us to remember."

I polished off the last of the whisky.

"You have your flock for your Christmas service, John. I

suspect they'll be here every year, now that they have someone to remember for them. And you can add one more to that, for as long as I live I too will be joining you in that remembrance."

I have kept that promise. I owed it to all the old soldiers.

I dance and sing and drum and dream with them and now I go to join them. I have served. I will serve, lost in the dance.

And the Dreaming Gods are singing where they lie.

"You kept the door open, now you've seen the dance," the old man said. "The baton has been passed. The tree was lost years ago, but the wood was saved, and reused. I think you know where. And now a wheel has turned. I am going, the house is waking up, and there's things you need to know."

Dave was thinking maybe he should just go back to sleep or maybe head for the whisky bottle, either activity made more sense than the current conversation but the other man had a grip on his arm and didn't look to be in the mood to let go.

The old man stared out at the windmills.

"You know, I haven't been happy for a long time. When I started on my path I truly thought that this was what I wanted. But I have seen everything I love wither and die. No matter how many platitudes I use to console myself, no matter how *cosmic* the thought that my molecules might see the death of the sun, I am lonely. I have been lonely for *so* long. But seeing these circles being drawn in the sky gives me hope. You don't have to be like me."

He let go of Dave's arm and turned to another page in his book.

CALX was the heading. The pictures showed a young man, bound to a burning wheel by hands and feet in a figure X. He was smiling.

"You see? More circles. *Calx* is Latin for Lime," he said. "In this case, it means calcination, or the process of purifying by heating. If you burn a body hot enough, it goes black, then, if you burn it even hotter, the ash turns white. Similarly, if you heat limestone, you'll produce a white powder that the Romans called *Calx Vita* or quicklime. This was considered a magical material, for, if you poured water on it, it gave out heat. Effectively, giving the heat back to the giver."

"And now I'm lost again," Dave said.

"This one's easy. Look at the picture. Fire purifies. Remember that. It's also a code that says, in effect, make quicklime. It will give heat back to the giver. And, beyond that, it symbolises the fact that the adept must purify his soul before continuing. Wheels within wheels yet again."

He tapped at the picture.

"This is from Greek mythology. *Ixion* was punished by Zeus. He tried to seduce *Hera*, and for his presumption was bound to a perpetual wheel of fire. But Ixion had seen the face of the Goddess, and although in eternal pain, was also eternally happy. Everything can be seen from two angles. Everything has at least two meanings. You will understand that, before the end."

He closed the book and looked Dave in the eye.

"You'll have to get inked of course, but that's no hardship. Maybe not a Balinese dancing girl though, eh?"

As he had the night before, Dave jerked as if he'd gotten an electric shock.

"How . . . ?"

The old man stopped him with a raise of his hand.

"The how isn't important. It's the why you need to concern yourself with. I could tell that you will see her again," he said. "But I am by no means sure that is true. What I do know is that nothing is ever wasted, not when doors like this one have been opened. There *are* wheels within wheels. My own wheels have finished turning in this meat suit I wear. I have been a ghost inside it for far too long. I will leave you, as I myself was left, with two words, and this book."

Turn again.

Dave looked down at the book as it was put in his hands. When he looked up again the old man was gone and there was no sign of him on the path in either direction.

He might have put the whole encounter down to another dream, but the book was real enough, the old leather still slightly warm to the touch where the old man had held it. He turned it over in his hands, expecting it too to fade.

First the marching figures, now this? What's going on around here?

One thing was for sure, Dave's daily routines were far out of joint. When he went back inside he looked to the mantel and Anne for stability.

"What do you think, sweetheart?" he said to the empty room. "Is your auld duffer really going cabin crazy?"

As soon as he said it, he took it to heart. Real or not, the old man had been the first person he'd spoken to for days; Anne didn't count. He needed something tangible to hold on to; a pint of beer was probably going to do the trick. It wasn't Wednesday but as his routines were off in any case he decided on a walk into Finsburgh. If nothing else a chinwag with some of the down-to-earth fishermen in the harbour pub would go a long way to settling him.

He took the leatherbound book inside and left it on the table beside his armchair, wondering whether it would still be there on his return. Then, putting it to the back of his mind, fetched his jacket and headed out onto the cliff path. He felt stiff from having spent the night sleeping outdoors on the bench but the walk quickly loosened up his old bones and once again the sea, sky and kittiwakes worked their magic. By the time he reached the town and took the steps down to the harbour he felt more like himself and the encounter with the old man had taken on a dream-like existence he thought he might be able to start forgetting.

He decided against a trip to the library and headed straight for the pub. The sights and sounds helped ground him in the here and now; the ting of the bell above the door, the tang of old leather and beer, the smell of polish on the bar-top and the aroma of cooking from the kitchen at the back. He stood at the bar while John poured a pint for him and looked up, into the long mirror that ran along the back. The old man from that morning sat in the seat by the window. The auld fellow saw Dave looking and raised a hand in a wave, showing Dave the stick figure . . . no left arm . . . tattooed on his palm. Dave turned to say hello.

The seat by the window was empty. When Dave turned back to the bar he looked in the mirror; the seat was still empty. He saw John looking at him, one eyebrow raised.

"What's up, auld yin? Somebody walk over your grave?"

"Just thought I saw somebody I knew," Dave replied, taking the beer and handing over a fiver. "Did you not see a wee auld man sitting by the window? Looks like death warmed up? Skin like an auld tree, blue eyes, a tattoo on his palm?"

"Auld Sandy Seton you mean?" John said. "If you saw anybody, it wasnae him. He was in just last week, but he'll no' be in again. He died last night. Are you sure you're okay? You look like you've seen a ghost."

Dave started to speak then thought better of it. He took to the beer to avoid having to reply. There was nothing he could say that would make any sense anyway.

Better to keep your mouth shut and be thought an idiot than to open it and prove it.

The landscape, sea and gulls didn't work their magic on him on the way back along the cliff; his mind was reeling with stick figures, conversations with dead men and worries about the possible onset of dementia. He fixed his gaze on his house as soon as it came into view, thankful that there was nobody sitting on the porch waiting for him, focussing on its solidity, the comfort of the known.

The first thing he looked for on entering was the book; part of him was hoping it wasn't there, another phantasm he could try to forget. But it sat where he'd left it on the table by his armchair. He ignored it and turned to the mantel.

"I'm having a bit of a day, sweetheart," he said to Anne's ashes, then saw that it wasn't over yet. A stick figure, six inches long, no left arm, was drawn on the face of the mirror above the urn. It was crudely done, with none of the refinement of the carvings he'd seen upstairs. As he walked over for a closer look, he saw with some horror that it had been done in coarse black ash.

His first thought was to check the urn. He said a silent prayer of thanks on finding that the seal was intact, Anne was intact. Then he checked the fireplace; he hadn't lit a fire since the Spring, and there was no sign that anyone had disturbed the soot in the chimney or around the hearth.

Somebody's playing silly buggers. And I'm not in the mood for it.

He went to the kitchen, dampened a cloth and returned to wipe the mirror clean. That done he checked the rest of the house but found nothing else amiss.

"I need to start locking the doors when I go out," he said to Anne.

She didn't reply.

The small routines involved in making lunch did little to calm him. After eating he checked his email, ignored the document containing the marching figures, and, with a drop of Scotch added to his coffee, finally turned his attention to the impossible book on the table.

The cover was a work of art in itself—calfskin over wood, with an embedded emblem intricately pierced and embroidered with thread and copper, depicting the serpent Ouroboros, circling the world and eating its tail. He ran his hands over the surface—smooth, and now cold to the touch. When he opened it a single folded sheet of good quality writing paper fell out. He opened it out and read.

"It was here before you, it will be here after you, but in the meantime it needs a keeper.

"Caves, chambers, trees or houses, there are places like this all over the world. Most people only know of them from whispered stories over campfires; tall tales told to scare the unwary. But some, those who suffer, some know better. They are drawn to the places where what ails them can be eased.

"If you have the will, the fortitude, you can peer into another life, where the dead are not gone, where you can see that they thrive and go on, in the dreams that stuff is made of.

"Your answers are in this book, if you can read it.

"Turn again."

It was signed and dated, Alexander Seton and yesterday's date.

He turned the paper over in his hands, looking for more but that is all there was. He got another surprise when he turned to the book itself.

"The Twelve Concordances of the Red Serpent. Transcribed from the original by Lieutenant Alexander Seton in the year of our Lord Eighteen Hundred and Ninety Eight."

It was in cursive, and in exactly the same hand as the note he'd read minutes before. If evidence was to be believed, Seton had been somewhere over a hundred and fifty years old at his death, and had written a note for him at some point after it.

What the hell is going on here?

He flipped through the book. There were plenty of mystical illustrations but the writing that accompanied them appeared to be in Latin. Dave had never progressed beyond Amo, Amas, Amat at school, and had no intention of learning now. He was about to put the book down when his gaze fell on something recognisable. It was one of the illustrations and showed a young man sitting in a room whose walls were covered in the now well known stick figures. On close inspection Dave saw that the youth was giving himself a tattoo on the forearm, a stick figure, one with no left arm.

He heard the old man's voice, as clearly as if it was being whispered in his ear.

"You'll have to get inked of course."

Nope. There's no way that's ever going to happen.

He spent the afternoon in his armchair with the television on, letting the inanities of what passed for daytime entertainment wash over him. He only looked up when he heard a familiar line. They were showing a movie clip. Bogart again, Casablanca this time.

"Where I'm going, you can't follow. What I've got to do, you can't be any part of."

As if in reply a loud scratching sound came from above him, somewhere upstairs. It sounded like it came from the attic. He went upstairs and stood below the hatchway waiting for a repeat of the noise, but none came although he smelled something, a tang with a hint of vinegar that faded as quickly as it had come. When he returned to the sitting room there was another ash figure drawn on the mirror, no left leg this time.

"Anne? Sweetheart? Is that you?" he whispered, not daring to hope.

The television screen flickered, showed a burst of white static and Bogart spoke again. Different movie, but the meaning seemed clear enough to Dave.

"You've got to convince me that you know what this is all about, that you aren't just fiddling around, hoping that it will all come out right in the end."

Dave's heart threatened to thud itself out of his chest.

He sat there for the rest of the afternoon and all through the evening, watching the screen, waiting for another sign and although there were no more strange occurrences, Dave felt a glimmer of purpose inside him that he hadn't felt in years.

You can see her again. The answers are in the book.

Latin or not Dave knew what he must do.

The next morning, after a fitful sleep, he began his study of *The Concordances*. His attack on it was two pronged; an attempt to decipher the dense Latin and, in the periods where his frustration got the better of him, study of the rows of stick figures. He worked with the television on in the background in the hope of a snippet of favourite dialogue or a scene from a mutually loved classic. But it appeared the point had been to get him to begin; there were no more messages.

The Latin proved impenetrable. He used several different auto-translate programs from the internet, with varying levels of failure and apart from some word fragments here and there could make little sense of the gibberish that resulted. He studied the illustrations, poring over the minutiae of each, even going as far as employing a magnifying glass in case he was missing some minor detail.

The answers are in this book, if you can read it.

It looked like the answers were staying where they were; none of Dave's attempts at comprehension led him anywhere except to abject frustration.

During the nights he dreamed again, but in the morning all he remembered were fragments, bits that he knew were important but still couldn't piece together.

Caelius tried to explain the Egyptian's death to Butto over a lunch of bread and cheese.

"You said that you knew of my study of the Elder cults," he began. "I will not bore you with the details of my searching—the task took many tedious years among dusty scrolls and clay tablets in ancient languages long since forgotten. But finally, I found something—something the Persians had discovered nearly a thousand years ago in a tomb in the ruins of Ur. They called it *Darbān* but it has had many names in many places—over the centuries, it has been called *Iog-Sototh, the Gatekeeper, the Dweller on the Threshold* and *the Veil of Fire* among a hundred—a thousand—other names. I know it as *The Opener of the Way.*"

"What does it open?" Butto asked.

"The veil—the curtain that separates us from the great mysteries. It is thin in some places, places where it is easier to cross over. I came close once, in a Maltese catacomb, where I saw then what I have now seen again—for this is such a place. The veil is thin here—very thin."

He told Butto of the manifestation in this plane of part of the *Sototh.*

"They are things of music and rhythm—that is how the Opener is called."

"So we have built our temple inside the older one—and we have angered an ancient god?" Butto asked, struggling to understand.

"No," Caelius said softly. "We have angered the guardian of the temple—an all too human guardian—we have angered the flautist, for it is only he who can call forth the Opener—and we must find him, before he sends us all the same way as your Egyptian."

Butto did not like Caelius' next suggestion.

"Over the wall? You want to send a hunting party into barbarian territory?"

"Only a small one—six men at the most. We need to find this flautist."

"I'll tell you this—none will go. These Gauls and Belgae are scared out of their wits as it is."

Caelius smiled grimly.

"I was not thinking of taking them—I will go—me, and the five who came up North with me. They are all my own men and have been with me for many years—they will go where I ask them to go, and fight when I ask them to fight."

"But it is madness—you do not know the territory."

"I am a Roman soldier, Butto. That has always been enough for me in the past—it will suffice now."

"The country is too open—you will be seen."

"We will leave at dusk, and we will be cloaked," Caelius said. "It is not as if we will be marching out in formation. Trust me—this will not be my first night raid."

"We can only hope it will not be your last." Butto replied.

Caelius spent much of the rest of the day in preparation. They would be travelling light—dark cloth cloaks and leather jerkins, each man armed only with a gladius, and no armour, no other metal of any kind that might give away their position by knocking against stone in the dark. Nor would they need provisions—the flautist would be close by, and they would only have a short time in which to find him if they were to prevent another man being lost this night. He briefed the men, although in truth there was not much to say. They were going over the wall to find the flautist. As a plan, the only thing it had going for it was simplicity.

As dusk fell Caelius and his men were ready to move.

They crept slowly down into the earthwork and up the other side before dropping down into what appeared to be little more than a wide expanse of moorland. The ground underfoot was a mixture of woody heathers, wet moss and scrawny dwarf birches, and there was just enough light to ensure that they did not go splashing around in any of the multitude of black stagnant ponds and rivulets that meandered through it.

It was a cloudy night—thin clouds that allowed occasional shards of moonlight that was perfect for their purposes. Caelius and his men tracked silently to and fro across the land within a mile of the wall, looking for any sign of Celtish incursion. Caelius had surmised that the flautist would need to be close enough to the fort for his purposes to be served, yet far enough away that the patrols would not be alerted. His theory was proved correct during their track through the second quadrant of their search area.

They heard them before they saw them, a muttering of soft voices that Caelius did not understand but knew immediately was Celtish. There appeared to be no more than four voices in the conversation. He held his men back—they wanted to rush the group immediately in a surprise attack, but Caelius needed to be sure that the flautist was present before they showed their hand.

He took it upon himself to creep forward, belly to the wet heather, moving as slowly and carefully as a cat on the hunt as he approached the voices. One of them sounded older; his voice was whispery, almost a croak. As Caelius got closer he saw there were indeed four in the group—three blue-painted warriors, naked above their short leather kilts, all holding tall bronze spears, and an old man, bent and wizened with age, the top of his head barely coming up to the chests of the warriors. But it was this older man who got all of Caelius' attention—even in the dim light he saw the short—no longer than a forefinger—white hollow bone that the man put to his lips. The sound of the bone flute carried across the moor like the cry of a nighthawk; the way was being opened again, and somewhere across the night on the guards' walk, a Roman soldier would be facing impending death.

Caelius couldn't afford to wait. He let out a cry that he hoped would alert his men to attack and leapt up out of the heather. He was on them and in the middle of their group before they realised he was there, and with the element of surprise on his side was able to slice his gladius clean through the neck of the closest Celt before the man even lifted his spear. The second Celt was faster and had his weapon up by the time Caelius spun round to face him—but a Celtish spear was no match for a Roman sword at such close range. It only took a second for Caelius to knock the bronze spearhead aside and plunge his blade deep into the man's chest. Then his men were there at his side and the other two Celtish warriors fell in seconds.

Only the old man was left standing. He opened his palms to show he was not armed. Caelius noted that the sound of the flute had stopped and there was no sign of the hollow white bone anywhere to be found.

Before he could call for a search to be made a spear thudded into the ground only feet away, coming from out of the night to the north—then another, this one landing in one of the black pools with a loud splash. There was no way of knowing how many Celts might be out there, even now advancing on their position.

"Back to the wall," Caelius said softly. "And quick about it, before they outflank us."

"What about the old man?" one of the others asked. "Kill him or bring him?"

"Bring him. We need that flute."

Then it was a run for safety, manhandling the old Celt with them all the way. All thought of caution was now gone as they splashed through pools and trudged through cloying bog that tugged at their ankles and threatened to have them stuck in the mire to be standing targets for any spear carriers who were following them.

As they reached the earthworks more spears thudded around them. Someone had taken note of their flight and had now spotted them. Caelius lost two men in the ditch—good men both, veterans of many campaigns—now taken in the back by a savage's spear. By the time Caelius pulled himself and the old man up onto the walkway his anger was up, and he was more than ready for a confrontation.

But the old man merely stood there, smiling and yammering in that singsong language of his that Caelius could not even begin to understand.

Butto arrived at his side. Caelius saw that most of the Sixth Cohort of Nervii was arranged up and down along the walkway and on the walls inside the fort. Some Celtish spears thudded in the ditch below them, but none reached even as far as the ground below their feet.

"I have the men out on the walk," Butto said. "Do you have your man?"

Caelius nodded toward the old Celt.

"The man, yes—the flute, no."

But when he looked again he saw that he was mistaken. The old Celt smiled, and pushed the white bone flute out of his mouth with his tongue—he'd had it secreted in his throat all this time. Before Caelius could make a move, the Celt started to play and after the first note, all thought of movement, of confrontation, was washed away from Caelius' mind, all rational thought was gone, lost to the call of the dance.

Lost.

On the third night of getting nowhere Dave slammed his fist hard on the table and swore loudly. The television screen flickered, and he got Bogie again.

"Now you are dangerous."

At the same moment the scratching in the attic started up again and this time it was continuous, almost rhythmic. Dave tapped his fingers on the table in time and, just like that, the answer, or one answer at least, came to him. The stick fingers weren't a code as such; they were something simpler. They were the markings of a rhythm, much like a musical stave but meant for a drummer.

As soon as the idea came to him he intuitively knew it was right. So, it seemed, did Bogie as the voice spoke again from the television.

"You won't need much of anybody's help. You're good."

Knowing the answer and being able to do anything with it proved to be two different things. Yes, he knew it was a rhythm of sorts but he needed a starting point to be able to work out the beats and times. It was now obvious to him that each stick figure represented a different beat but it wasn't until he realised that each of the figures represented eight beats to the bar . . . a head being two, a body also two and four limbs, one beat each . . . that he felt he might be getting somewhere.

Then it became a matter of trial and error. He opened up his laptop and read along a line of the stick figures in the document.

No limbs, no limbs, no head, no head, left arm gone, left leg gone, no legs, no head.

Four beats, four beats, six beats, six beats, seven beats, seven beats, six beats, six beats. He tapped them out on the table with his fingertips. There was a two second pause and then the scratching in the attic answered.

No limbs, no limbs, no head, no head, left arm gone, left leg gone, no legs, no head.

The television also had an opinion although this time Dave couldn't even guess at its intention.

"Their flesh is too much like the flesh of men, and their perfume has the rotten sweetness of corruption."

All he knew was that he was getting somewhere. He tapped out more of the rhythm.

No left leg, no head, no limbs, no right arm, no arms, no head and no legs.

Seven beats, six beats, four beats, seven beats, six beats, six beats, six beats.

The scratching in the attic came in on the fourth bar, keeping time with him. Dave tapped, the thing in the attic scratched. Dave stamped his feet in time. Despite himself he used one hand to move forward between the pages of the document that showed the ranks of figures while his other hand, clench in a fist now, pounded on the table. The beat went up a notch, took on an almost choral quality that echoed and rang around the house.

The room swam in his vision, getting darker, dimmer. Guttural voices rose to join the rhythm and from somewhere distant, as if heard in a stiff wind, he heard the keening of the local kittiwakes join in, in time.

The laptop dropped to the floor unheeded as he brought his hands together in clapping.

No limbs, no limbs, no head, no head, left arm gone, left leg gone, no legs, no head.

It felt like the top of his head was going to lift off as the beat grew and grew, the house shook and swayed as if caught in a swell and the voices and the drumming and the clapping and the stomping rose to a frenzy.

The darkness swallowed up the light leaving Dave alone in a vast cavern of emptiness where all that mattered was the beat.

Stick figures ran there, all dancing, each of them lost.

Lost to the dance.

Once again white, dancing motes of light filled the Roman's vision, and the flute rose to a cacophony of wails and cries, as if many were joined in the playing. A fog came up, seeping from the ground below them, and a black vortex spun, and grew, and began to suck. Some of the men tried to run, but the vortex was greedy and it crept along the wall—where it passed, the men wailed, and fell, heart-struck, even as their very essences were sucked away, stick figures dancing into the void beyond the veil.

Caelius felt the vortex tug at him, felt its seduction. But he had felt it before—felt it, and resisted. His earlier words to Butto came back to him.

"I am a Roman soldier, Butto. That has always been enough in the past—it will suffice now."

He managed to turn towards the old man—the Celt's smile faded.

He did not expect me to be able to resist.

That thought gave him even more impetus, and he was able to step forward and grab the old man by the throat, choking off the fluting.

But the damage had been done—the vortex did not fade, and the men kept falling beneath it. The ground below Caelius' feet thrummed with the power of the open gate. And he knew what had to be done.

He grabbed the flute from the old man, clubbed the Celt hard on the chin and, with the man slung over his shoulder, headed at speed for the only place where he thought the vortex might be stopped—the old temple in the underpinnings of the fort.

Now that he had an inkling of what he was dealing with, he headed straight for the Temple chamber. The darkness was waiting for his return. The black tear opened again in the air above the centre of the chamber, accompanied by what sounded like the ripping of paper.

A single black egg dropped out of it, a spinning globule no bigger than a thumb, and hung there, quivering. A rainbow aura danced over it, and ever so slowly it split and became two, oily sheen running over their sleek black surfaces. They hummed to themselves, a high singing that was taken up and amplified by an answering whine from the surrounding rock itself. A drumbeat started up to accompany it.

No limbs, no limbs, no head, no head, left arm gone, left leg gone, no legs, no head.

As two eggs became four, the whole chamber rocked from side to side in rhythm.

The dance had begun again.

Caelius had come down here without any firm idea as to how to approach the problem—faced with the shimmering, dancing eggs he felt small and lost, all too aware of the minuscule part he played in the great scheme of things, in a dance that never began and never ended. All he could do for the moment was watch—watch, and hope for enlightenment.

He heard a loud, frightened gasp to his left, and turned, knife in hand, almost expecting an attack. The old Celt was getting to his feet. It seemed to take him a great effort to drag his eyes from the swirling, cavorting, halving, eggs.

"This is my place now. This is my land again," the Celt said in halting Latin, "I will guard. I will serve."

Eight black eggs hung impossibly in the air between the two men, oily and glistening, thrumming in time with the vibration from the walls that was getting ever louder, ever more insistent. Caelius had to resist a sudden urge to start clapping and stamping in time to the beat.

Thick fog glowed in an aurora of rainbow colour and swirled angrily above them, creating a false sky in the ceiling of the darkened chamber.

Eight eggs became sixteen, and then thirty-two just seconds later, all clustered in a tight ball that spun lazily in the air. The walls of rock were changing too—the stone had become noticeably thinner, almost translucent and swirling rainbow fog clearly moved through them. The walls thinned further, almost ghostly now, then vanished completely until there was only the dark and the darker eggs hanging in it—sixty-four now, and singing louder.

The dust and dirt on the floor underfoot started to tremble and shake, then, as if taken by a wind, rose in a tight funnel spiralling up toward the hanging eggs, faster and faster still. The eggs sucked up the material and sang louder, as if requesting more.

Caelius felt the vortex suck at him again—the gate was opening wider. There were too many eggs to count now—into the hundreds. They almost filled the space in the chamber, their song rising higher, the beat and thrum of the rhythm filling Caelius's head, and the dancing rainbow colours filling his eyes with blue and green and gold and wonderment.

His whole body shook, vibrating with the rhythm. His head swam, and it seemed as if everything melted and ran. The scene receded into a great distance until it was little more than a pinpoint in a blanket of darkness, and he was alone, in a vast cavern of emptiness where nothing existed save the dark and the pounding.

And then there was light.

He saw stars—vast swathes of gold and blue and silver, all dancing in great purple and red clouds that spun webs of grandeur across unending vistas. Shapes moved in and among the nebulae; dark, wispy shadows casting a pallor over everything they covered— shadows that capered and whirled as the dance grew ever more frenetic. Caelius felt buffeted, as if by a strong, surging tide, but as the beat grew ever stronger he cared little. He gave himself to it, lost in the dance, lost in the stars.

He did not know how long he wandered in the space between. He forgot myself, forgot the Empire's business, forgot the old Celt, dancing in the vastness where only rhythm mattered.

Dave came out of it lying on his back, looking up at the hatchway to the attic. It had been opened. The blackness above seemed to beckon him upwards. It was a voice from the television that made him turn away and head downstairs.

It wasn't Bogie this time, but Bergman.

"I know how you feel about me, but I'm asking you to put your feelings aside for something more important."

"Anne? Sweetheart? I don't understand. What am I to do?"

But once again it seemed that the lesson had been given, even if he didn't understand it, it was all he was going to get. The house fell quiet around him.

I'm getting somewhere. I only wish I knew where.

Dog-tired, he trudged to his bedroom and fell, face down on the mattress. He was asleep a minute later.

Caelius may never have returned from the dance had the old man not brought him back. He heard a noise, something not of the dance, and was curious enough to follow it. A face slowly came into focus, as if coming at him from a great distance, and a voice spoke—shouted—as if trying to speak to him in a great wind.

"This is not for you, Roman! This is my land, my place to serve."

It was the thought of his duty that brought Caelius back—back from a place where humankind was as insignificant as one of those motes of dancing dust. But when he finally managed to focus fully on the old man, he could see that the Celt was now as far gone from humanity as the stars among which he had been dancing.

The Celt's head looked misshapen and deformed, as if his brain had grown too large to be contained in his skull and was threatening to expunge itself. It was a second before Caelius realised what he was seeing—the Celt was growing horns that were already spiralling out in bloody protrusions from his skull. His hands had taken on a peculiar rough aspect, as had his feet, looking more like course, matted hair than skin. The Celt's left hand in particular bothered Caelius—it had thickened and hardened into black cuticle; it looked like it wanted to become a cloven hoof. More of the thick wiry hair ran, not just over the old man's face but up and down both his arms. The Celt went to stand at the edge of the hanging batch of eggs then, without a pause, stepped inside and quickly moved to the centre where he raised his hands until they seemed to be engulfed in the mass. Caelius could hardly see him inside the swirling aurora of dancing colour.

The eggs danced faster—thousands of them filling the chamber with song and dance that he had to fight to resist. The Celt sank his hands completely into them.

"I will serve," he shouted.

The drumbeat in the chamber got louder. Dust disturbed by the vibration drifted down from the roof to fall around them. Caelius staggered, almost fell, buffeted by a cold wind that blew a gale through the chamber.

The floor bucked and swayed, and once again Caelius almost fell.

The myriad of eggs popped, burst and disappeared as if they had never been there at all. Dancing fog swirled, a dark funnel that brought more howling, screaming wind.

The old Celt screamed.

"This place is mine."

Everything went black and a thunderous blast came down like a hammer from above, driving Caelius down into a place where he dreamed of empty spaces filled with oily, glistening bubbles. They popped and spawned yet more bubbles, then even more, until he swam in a swirling sea of colours.

Lost.

Dave woke some time later with a start, brought awake by the sound of renewed scratching in the attic.

No limbs, no limbs, no head, no head, left arm gone, left leg gone, no legs, no head.

Still half-asleep, he tapped out his reply on the bed's headboard.

Four beats, four beats, six beats, six beats, seven beats, seven beats, six beats, six beats.

The scratching from above grew more insistent, more rapid. Dave tried to follow the rhythm of it but his still-befuddled brain couldn't keep up. He rose from bed and went out to stand below the still-open hatchway.

"What do you want from me?" he said.

He smelled vinegar again, stronger than before. Something moved above him, heavy, as if slumping. It scratched.

No limbs, no limbs, no head, no head, left arm gone, left leg gone, no legs, no head.

"I hope you know what you're doing sweetheart," Dave whispered, and started up the ladder.

He poked his head up above the hatch. To switch on the attic light he'd have to go all the way up and inside, and his legs were refusing to help him with that; it was all he could do to hold himself upright on the ladder. He peered, trying to make sense of the shifting shadows.

The tang was stronger still here and there was more than vinegar in it. It carried an almost sweet, cloying smell.

"Their flesh is too much like the flesh of men, and their perfume has the rotten sweetness of corruption."

The stick figure carvings on the beams had returned. They glowed red as if burning, and the light they gave off allowed Dave a look at the thing that lay slumped in the angle where the roof sloped down to meet the attic floor.

It was almost all bone, a stick figure brought to some grotesque semblance of life, a skeleton in its most basic form with a single rigid backbone fused in one knotted piece, rudimentary limbs with no elbow or knee joints and a head too large for the proportions of its body. It had horns, no, more like antlers, growing up and out from the forehead even as Dave watched.

Its left arm was missing and when it turned towards him it had no face, only circular black holes where eyes and mouth should be.

And yet it looked directly at Dave.

And it knows me.

Ten seconds later, with barely a conscious thought of having done it, Dave was back downstairs, a large measure of Scotch in hand. He sat at the kitchen table with *The Concordances* open in front of him, and this time he was starting to make sense of the snippets and snatches of words he had translated from the Latin.

Service it said. *Dialogue* it promised, an eternity of it should it be desired. But service was the important thing, service to the new master of the house, service to the place of dreams made real.

Yes, he could see Anne again, or at least know that he was talking to her and that she was hearing. But for that prize, fealty was demanded, and tribute must be made. He heard the old man's words again.

You'll have to get inked, of course.

The thing in the attic scratched.

No head, no head, no left arm.

Dave remembered the old man in the bar mirror, raising his hand, showing his palm, and knew what he had to do. He went to a cupboard and fetched a bottle of India Ink and a sewing needle. He swabbed the needle with whisky and rubbed some on his forearm just above his wrist. He was about to make the first prick when the television came on without warning, white static, Anne's voice.

"Where I'm going, you can't follow. What I've got to do, you can't be any part of."

"But I can," Dave whispered. "All I have to do is serve. We can have eternity."

She wasn't having it.

"You want to feel sorry for yourself, don't you? With so much at stake, all you can think of is your own feelings."

"I thought this was what you wanted? What we both wanted?"

Before he got a reply the thing in the attic scratched again, loudly and insistently.

No limbs, no limbs, no head, no head, left arm gone, left leg gone, no legs, no head.

He heard a clatter and a thud and knew immediately that the dead bones had left the attic and come down out of the hatchway. The scratching now came from the hallway above him.

It was getting closer.

His vision swam. For a few short seconds he was Roman again.

He woke in the dark, lying on cold rock.

He had to feel his way to the exit by touch, and on finally making his way out of the chamber found that the rest of the way up through the fort was lit by dim moonlight.

The Sixth Cohort of Nervii—what remained of them—stood on the top of the wall and as Caelius looked out to the north it was to see a rag-tag band of Celts fading back into the misty moorland beyond.

"I have lost a third of my men—but we have won," Butto said. He had a long cut from forehead to chin, but he was smiling. "By Jupiter, we have done it."

"No," Caelius replied quietly. "I do not think we have—and I do not think we ever will. We do not belong here. You will realise that for yourself soon enough."

He still had the bone flute in his hand. He broke it in three pieces and threw it into the ditch. When he turned away, he was already wondering whether his home beyond the wall of Hadrian was far enough south—whether he would ever be far enough south.

Anne spoke from the television. Dave heard urgency in her voice.

"I can't fight it anymore. I ran away from you once. I can't do it again. I don't know what's right any longer. You have to think for both of us. For all of us."

Dave was thinking, of servitude and eternity, of love lost, love found. He thought of Casablanca, of Bogart, then of Sam Spade and of a falcon.

The dreams that stuff is made of.

He heard the clatter of bones on the stairs, the insistent scratching on the walls, demanding fealty, demanding service.

No limbs, no limbs, no head, no head, left arm gone, left leg gone, no legs, no head.

It held no compulsion for him. He dropped the needle and ink on the table and turned all his attention to the television.

"You've been trying to tell me all this time, haven't you, sweetheart? You said I was to do the thinking for both of us. Well,

I've done some since then and it all adds up to one thing. Where I'm going, you can't follow. What I've got to do, you can't be any part of. But we already have eternity . . . we've always had that. And we don't need anyone, or anything's permission."

The scratching got louder, became wild, frenzied thumping. The house shook with the rage of it but Dave felt calm wash over him as he took *The Concordances* to the fireplace and began to systematically tear pages from the book and crumple them in the hearth. He heard the bony thing behind him, in the doorway now, pounding on the walls with a skeletal fist, but it held no power over him.

He got the matchbox from the mantel, bent, and set the pages of the book alight, placing the rest of it atop the growing flames. The fire spread fast, lapping up the walls on either side of the fireplace but Dave only smiled.

He gently lifted Anne's urn from its position and carried it out of the house. Everything he owned burned behind him.

He only looked back once. A stick figure stood in the doorway, no left arm, high antlers outlined black with fire behind. It pounded against the door frame.

No limbs, no limbs, no head, no head, left arm gone, left leg gone, no legs, no head.

The house fell in around it and flames danced in the night.

Dave turned away and went to the cliff edge. Dawn rose amid the offshore windmills.

"Turn again," he whispered, broke the seal on the urn, and released Anne to fly with the kittiwakes, where he knew he would always find her.

"Here's looking at you, kid."

a knot within a knot

jason parent

part III

Idon't know how long I've been in the loo. At some point, I must have fainted.

All is quiet outside the small cabin and has been for many hours. It's been at least half a day since I heard the last scream.

And still I wait. My throat is so dry that if I had a toilet with any water in it, I would have drunk from it already. I've tried the sink, but nothing comes out. *Why hasn't anyone found us yet?*

My phone lost its charge even before I ran from that—whatever *that* was, some kind of reindeer or elk but much bigger than anything roaming wild back home. I shudder as I recall how it turned those seated in front of me into human pincushions. That was no animal. That was something all evil.

Whatever came afterward, I dared not venture to see. I awoke to fresh screams, more pounding at the door, and the bitter taste of ash. Or perhaps I imagined that last bit. Regardless, whatever wanted into the loo had my back to contend with as I braced it shut, clamped my hands over my ears, and to my shame, left the other passengers to their fates.

Now, no more knocks come to my door.

I have no idea whether any of my hundreds of texts made it through to my husband. Between the storm and what I guess to be the remoteness of our crash site because of all the trees we hit as we plummeted earthward, I doubt I ever had a signal. Dave must be worried sick.

But I am alive. I press my ear against the door. By the sound of it, I may be the only one yet living. I chuckle nervously as my hand rests on the handle, and my mind replays my favorite Humphrey Bogart quote: "Things are never so bad they can't be made worse."

I take a deep breath, slowly pull the handle, and push the door. It doesn't budge. My breaths come a little quicker as I rest my shoulder against the door and push harder. The door creaks like a house settling against the pressure but remains closed. *What if I can't get out? What if there's something still out there that wants in?*

a knot within a knot

I slip back onto the toilet seat and listen. I didn't make a lot of noise, but in the dead silence that lingers outside the loo, it might as well have been a trumpet blare. With my hands folded over my bouncing knees, I wait for a response.

None comes. As my gaze rises to the door, I read the word Occupied and realize the door is still locked. As I slide the latch to the left, it clicks loudly. Again, I pause and wait to see if my actions cause reactions. Finally, I summon the courage to try the door again.

It creaks open, and I peer through a narrow slit. At most, I can see only a few rows of chairs and a portion of the aisle, all of which appear empty. But the air is full of moisture, hanging heavily as if humid but chilled and carrying with it a rotten odor like that of a slaughterhouse. I pull my blouse up over my nose and open the door wider, leaning my shoulder against it and chancing a better look while remaining always ready to retreat quickly back into my throne room.

Seeing nothing and no one, I step into the aisle. The odor is so strong now that it permeates my shirt. My nose crinkles as I hold in my disgust.

A *thud* comes from behind me, and I jump as something brushes against my heel. I whip around to find a water bottle rolling away from me and the streak of something small, brown, and furry—a chipmunk or a field mouse—dart out of sight behind the flight attendants' curtain.

I take long breaths to slow my heart before facing forward and taking in the rest of the plane. I kept my seat through the crash, somehow survived unharmed and relatively sane, and only went mental when a man, a *giant*, lifted the plane and sent that great black monster into the cabin. My mind unraveled completely when it prodded passengers with its antlers and crushed them beneath its weight. *What did I do to escape that beast? Who did I cause to be hurt?*

I shake off the reverie. It is not the time or the place for guilt and grief. I'd have plenty of time for that if I made it out of here alive.

I search for the water bottle near my feet, find it, and pour its contents down my scratched throat. I cough and sputter, having swallowed too much too quickly.

Ahead of me, no more than a dozen rows remain intact. Ahead

of them, chairs form twisted shapes akin to garbage art with hints of Picasso cubism, where there are any seats left at all. Beyond that, the remainder of the plane is like an empty pill capsule, broken in half with its other end missing. And everywhere, all around me, streaks of a nearly black substance coat fabric and aluminum alike.

Not a single person or even a part of a person remains. *If everyone is dead, where are the bodies?*

I walk down the aisle until my feet hit solid earth. A meadow sits before me, and beyond it, a gigantic dome spreads over acres and acres of what has to be forest, which I judge by the tips of large pines that jab out of the dome's apparently tangible surface to pierce the bright-blue sky. Something about that massive ebony shape reminds me of that old film *The Blob*, and I try not to imagine what it might be like for one trapped inside it. Darkness and gloom is not supposed to have a definite shape. Just gazing upon it sets my heart palpitating and my stomach roiling. *I will not be going in there.*

As foreboding as the shaped darkness may be, the dread it instills pales in comparison to the terror of the crash and what came after. Since the darkness doesn't appear to be moving, I take in the remainder of my surroundings. Mountains range in the distance to my left and to my right. I circle the wreckage, searching for a decline. A part of my mind has apparently already decided that the best way out of here is down.

Only now do I notice the neck pillow somehow still cradling my neck. How it somehow maintained its perch through all that happened strikes me as just about the funniest thing I have seen in all my life. I laugh long and hard, so much that tears fill my eyes.

The shrill notes of a flute being played somewhere in the distance cuts short my mad laughter. A drumbeat follows, but I cannot place where the sounds are coming from.

I watch the dome and squint as I catch what seems to be a vertical slit in the air half the distance between the crash site and the darkened forest. I assume the sunlight illuminating the clearing is reflecting off some surface, or more likely, the change in lighting has summoned spots before my eyes. I raise a hand over them like a visor and blink my vision clear. But when I look again, the slit is bigger, and the music, speaker-less yet in surround sound, grows louder.

A small black orb drops from the black hole or whatever it is, and I try again to clear my eyes, this time rubbing them with the heels of my palms. But the effort only makes the blurriness worse, because when I look again, there are two of the damn egg things spinning in front of me, shimmering with rainbows in that somewhat-beautiful way oil slicks do. I am of no mind to appreciate their beauty, however—the beauty of my hallucinations.

As the earth under my feet trembles, sending vibrations through me that make goose bumps rise on my arms, I rub my eyes again. The vibrations increase as the music crescendos, and I keep my eyes shut.

I am alone. I am infinitesimal. In God's great plan, I do not factor.

My head spins, and I sway on my feet, overcome by a sensation of utter bleakness, a despair that commands me to lie down and die just like I feel—*no, somehow know*—all the others in the plane did before me. *Who am I to escape a god's will? Who am I to fight elemental and eternal truths?* I crouch and bury my head in my hands.

As I think to lie down with no intention of ever getting back up, the music and shaking stop. Like a wave of nausea passing, so do my ill feelings. Bogart's voice echoes in my brain. *"I should never have switched from scotch to martinis."*

I rise and look toward the dome. The orb things and their accompanying rift in space are gone, as if they never existed. *Because they never did exist.*

Instead, a little girl with pigtails stands where the mirage was, her gaze fixed on me. I shake my head, half expecting the girl to vanish when I straighten. But she remains standing there, her arms outstretched.

"Hey there!" I call as I slowly close the distance to avoid scaring her off. I feel suddenly lighter, not alone. "Are you okay?"

The little girl doesn't answer. She drops her arms but shows no signs of an intent to flee.

As I get within a few feet, I slow even more. The toddler's skin is pale, almost with a greenish tint, which I assume must be another play of the light off the vibrant grass at our feet.

"Hi," I say again.

The girl just looks up at me, pouting. Her eyes are yellow, like those of a meth addict.

"Are you hurt?" I squat next to her, thinking she might have jaundice or some similar affliction but lacking the qualifications to make such a diagnosis. "Are you sick?"

Her chin presses against her shirt as a frown spreads over her chubby cheeks.

"I'm Anne." I extend my hand. "I'm going to walk down this mountain. Would you like to come with me?"

The little girl looks up at that and fixes me with a smile.

I gasp and lurch away. I could have sworn I saw a mouth full of teeth, far too many for any toddler and much more triangular in shape.

Her smile vanishes, and a sneer replaces it. Her yellow eyes glower at me, her pupils like black slits. *Like little rifts in space.* And she never blinks, which makes little sense until I realize she has no eyelids.

I take a hesitant step backward then another.

The little girl's glower becomes something more, something worse, as if her shark-like grin grows in equal parts to my discomfort. In a voice much too low to belong to a child and much too gravelly to belong to a human, the little girl says, "You will take me down this mountain, or I will leave you at the mercy of something worse."

I follow the girl's gaze. She is looking off in the distance, toward a pink, wavering light in the wood line. I'm not sure what I'm seeing. At first, it looks like a living shadow with a pink flame blazing in its center. It's not a shadow, though. It glides, almost weightless, but there is substance to it. The strange and terrible light reveals cracks and blisters all over its charcoal flesh.

The little girl-thing titters. "There are things in this world who serve powers older and more terrible than I."

Malevolence and hatred dance with a sense of awe in her tone. Maybe I'm mistaken . . . I hope I am, but she seems afraid of the being with the fire burning in its chest. I step farther away.

I shudder at the wrongness of the child that stands before me. Despite the fear and unease that the toddler stirs in me, the monster that approaches scares me more. It strides toward us, like death itself. I retreat closer to the lesser of two evils.

"Yesssss," the girl-thing hisses. "Come. I know the way." She reaches for me.

I swallow the lump in my throat and take her outstretched hand. *Its* hand. Its flesh is cold and slimy against my palm. I try to ignore it as we begin our walk, if only to stay alive a little longer, wondering if lidless eyes ever sleep.

Subscribe to Crystal Lake Publishing's Dark Tide series for updates, specials, behind-the-scenes content, and a special selection of bonus stories
- http://eepurl.com/hKVGkr

THE END?

Not if you want to dive into more of the Dark Tide series.

Check out our amazing website and online store
or download our latest catalog here.
https://geni.us/CLPCatalog

We always have great new projects and content on the website to dive into, as well as a newsletter, behind the scenes options, social media platforms, our own dark fiction shared-world series and our very own webstore. Our webstore even has categories specifically for KU books, non-fiction, anthologies, and of course more novels and novellas.

About the Authors

Jason Parent is an author of horror, thrillers, mysteries, science fiction and dark humor, though his many novels, novellas, and short stories tend to blur the boundaries between genres. From his EPIC and eFestival Independent Book Award finalist first novel, *What Hides Within*, to his widely applauded police procedural/supernatural thriller, *Seeing Evil*, to his fast and furious sci-fi horror, *The Apocalypse Strain*, Jason's work has won him praise from both critics and fans of diverse genres alike. He currently lives in Massachusetts, surrounded by chewed furniture thanks to his corgi and mini Aussie pups.

Curtis M. Lawson is a weird fiction author, editor, comic creator, poet, podcaster, and table top game developer. His work ranges from technicolor pulp adventures to bleak cosmic horror.
Curtis resides on the outskirts of Providence Rhode Island. He is the host of the Wyrd Transmissions podcast and runs Gallows Whisper, an imprint of Weird House Press.

William Meikle is a Scottish writer, now living in Canada, with over thirty novels published in the genre press and more than 300 short story credits in thirteen countries. He has books available from a variety of publishers including Dark Regions Press and Severed Press and his work has appeared in a large number of professional anthologies and magazines. He lives in Newfoundland with whales, bald eagles and icebergs for company. When he's not writing he drinks beer, plays guitar, and dreams of fortune and glory.

Readers . . .

Thank you for reading *An Unholy Triquetra*. We hope you enjoyed this 9th book in our Dark Tide series.

If you have a moment, please review *An Unholy Triquertra* at the store where you bought it.

Help other readers by telling them why you enjoyed this book. No need to write an in-depth discussion. Even a single sentence will be greatly appreciated. Reviews go a long way to helping a book sell, and is great for an author's career. It'll also help us to continue publishing quality books. You can also share a photo of yourself holding this book with the hashtag #IGotMyCLPBook!

Thank you again for taking the time to journey with Crystal Lake Publishing.

Visit our Linktree page for a list of our social media platforms. https://linktr.ee/CrystalLakePublishing

Our Mission Statement:

Since its founding in August 2012, Crystal Lake Publishing has quickly become one of the world's leading publishers of Dark Fiction and Horror books in print, eBook, and audio formats.

While we strive to present only the highest quality fiction and entertainment, we also endeavour to support authors along their writing journey. We offer our time and experience in non-fiction projects, as well as author mentoring and services, at competitive prices.

With several Bram Stoker Award wins and many other wins and nominations (including the HWA's Specialty Press Award), Crystal Lake Publishing puts integrity, honor, and respect at the forefront of our publishing operations.

We strive for each book and outreach program we spearhead to not only entertain and touch or comment on issues that affect our readers, but also to strengthen and support the Dark Fiction field and its authors.

Not only do we find and publish authors we believe are destined for greatness, but we strive to work with men and woman who endeavour to be decent human beings who care more for others than themselves, while still being hard working, driven, and passionate artists and storytellers.

Crystal Lake Publishing is and will always be a beacon of what passion and dedication, combined with overwhelming teamwork and respect, can accomplish. We endeavour to know each and every one of our readers, while building personal relationships with our authors, reviewers, bloggers, podcasters, bookstores, and libraries.

We will be as trustworthy, forthright, and transparent as any business can be, while also keeping most of the headaches away from our authors, since it's our job to solve the problems so they can stay in a creative mind. Which of course also means paying our authors.

We do not just publish books, we present to you worlds within your world, doors within your mind, from talented authors who sacrifice so much for a moment of your time.

There are some amazing small presses out there, and through collaboration and open forums we will continue to support other presses in the goal of helping authors and showing the world what quality small presses are capable of accomplishing. No one wins when a small press goes down, so we will always be there to support hardworking, legitimate presses and their authors. We don't see Crystal Lake as the best press out there, but we will always strive to be the best, strive to be the most interactive and grateful, and even blessed press around. No matter what happens over time, we will also take our mission very seriously while appreciating where we are and enjoying the journey.

What do we offer our authors that they can't do for themselves through self-publishing?

We are big supporters of self-publishing (especially hybrid publishing), if done with care, patience, and planning. However, not every author has the time or inclination to do market research, advertise, and set up book launch strategies. Although a lot of authors are successful in doing it all, strong small presses will always be there for the authors who just want to do what they do best: write.

What we offer is experience, industry knowledge, contacts and trust built up over years. And due to our strong brand and trusting fanbase, every Crystal Lake Publishing book comes with weight of respect. In time our fans begin to trust our judgment and will try a new author purely based on our support of said author.

With each launch we strive to fine-tune our approach, learn from our mistakes, and increase our reach. We continue to assure our authors that we're here for them and that we'll carry the weight of the launch and dealing with third parties while they focus on their strengths—be it writing, interviews, blogs, signings, etc.

We also offer several mentoring packages to authors that include knowledge and skills they can use in both traditional and self-publishing endeavours.

We look forward to launching many new careers.

This is what we believe in. What we stand for. This will be our legacy.

Welcome to Crystal Lake Publishing— Tales from the Darkest Depths.